James J. Moriarty

The Keys of the Kingdom

James J. Moriarty

The Keys of the Kingdom

ISBN/EAN: 9783337191528

Printed in Europe, USA, Canada, Australia, Japan

Cover: Foto ©Andreas Hilbeck / pixelio.de

More available books at **www.hansebooks.com**

THE KEYS OF THE KINGDOM;

OR,

THE UNFAILING PROMISE.

BY THE

REV. JAMES J. MORIARTY, LL.D.,

Pastor of St. John the Evangelist's Church, Syracuse, N. Y., and Author of "Stumbling-Blocks made Stepping-Stones on the Road to the Catholic Faith," "All for Love; or, From the Manger to the Cross," "Wayside Pencillings," etc. etc.

"I say to thee: That thou art Peter; and upon this rock I will build my Church, and the gates of hell shall not prevail against it. And I will give to thee the Keys of the Kingdom of Heaven." —ST. MATTHEW, xvi. 18, 19.

NEW YORK:

THE CATHOLIC PUBLICATION SOCIETY CO.,

9 BARCLAY STREET.

LONDON: BURNS & OATES.

TO

Saint Peter,

THE CHIEF OF THE APOSTOLIC BAND,

THE CONFIRMER OF HIS BRETHREN,

THE CENTRE OF UNITY,

The Rock upon which Christ built His Church,

TO WHOM WERE CONFIDED

The Keys of the Kingdom of Heaven,

AND

THE CARE OF SHEPHERDS AND SHEEP,

THIS LITTLE WORK IS REVERENTLY DEDICATED

WITH THE HOPE AND PRAYER

THAT THROUGH HIS INTERCESSION MANY SOULS NOW WAN-

DERING IN THE MAZES OF ERROR MAY BE BROUGHT

INTO

The One Fold under the One Shepherd.

CONTENTS.

INTRODUCTION.

DISTINGUISHED English author lately published a most interesting work, under the title *Is Life Worth Living?* which has been widely read, dealing, as it does, with a question that every thoughtful man has asked himself, especially in moments of sadness or deep meditation. This stirring question is so closely connected with another of no less import that if we answer one adequately we cover the ground occupied by the other: Is Religion worth Studying?

If life be really worth living, it is only because of religion, the key it affords to the mysteries of life, the motives of action which it furnishes, the innumerable aids it supplies, the consolations it gives, and the grand, well-founded hopes it holds out of a brighter, undying life in the future.

If we be not mistaken as to the drift of Mr. Mallock's work, we believe ·that this is the conclusion to which he wishes to draw his readers; but he merely points it out and leaves to others the task of farther development.

Though not gifted with his magic pen nor able to charm by any of his many graces of style, we purpose examining, in our own humble way, this most important of living questions, hoping and praying that our simple line of argument, couched in plain, heartfelt words, may, in some measure, help to make life worth living to some earnest, anxious souls struggling forward towards the light that beams from the everlasting shore.

We shall first strive to answer the leading question, "Is Religion worth Studying?" If so, which religion? By whom was the true religion founded; what rule of faith was laid down; what marks, notes, or characteristics distinguish the one true Church from all others, so that it can be easily discerned by any man of earnest, inquiring mind and of prayerful habit?

These shining marks of the one true faith are like wonderful gems, which are so resplendent in themselves that they need not the enchasing of human eloquence nor the adornment which rhetoric might be able to furnish. In this case truly is "beauty unadorned adorned the most." For, as the late Cardinal Wiseman remarked, "truth is a gem which need not be enchased, which, faultless and cloudless, may be held up to the pure bright light, on any side, in any direction, and will everywhere display the same purity and soundness and beauty."

Christ has adorned His Spouse—His Church—with four most brilliant gems "of purest ray serene," that no

"Dark, unfathomed caves of ocean bear,"

but which have been exposed to a critical world for nineteen centuries, placed in most trying lights, subjected to the most crucial tests, and yet no mists of error nor darkness of heresy or infidelity have been able to cast the slightest cloud on their dazzling brightness. These gems, that shine forth so grandly from the bosom of Christ's spotless One as to be seen by all men whose sight is purified by studious inquiry and enlightening grace, are Unity, Sanctity, Catholicity, and Apostolicity.

In treating of these characteristics of the Catholic faith we shall necessarily have to refer to opposing systems of religion and to their manifest lack of these shining qualities by which Christ wished His Church to be for ever distinguished. Truth is not always agreeable, yet, for the sake of immortal souls that are perishing for want of the light and are living in "the darkness of the shadow of death," it should be told plainly yet kindly. Hence, in whatever we have written in this book, it is certainly not our intention to offend; and when we have had something to say that might appear harsh to those not of the household of · faith, we have endeavored to select the opinions of non-Catholic writers, and let those speak who cannot be accused of any partiality towards our Holy Mother the Church.

It is surely the prompting of Christian charity on the part of him who firmly and unhesitatingly believes that he is in possession of the only true, saving faith, and who has a deep, abiding love for his fellow-men, more especially for his fellow-citizens of a great and free republic, to endeavor to lead them to the attainment of the same light and knowledge and to the participation of the same incomparable happiness.

It would be false liberality and still more false charity for such a one to allow himself to be dragged down from the sublime height of divine truth on which he stands to the level of the men, in the present age, who are without any Christian faith. It is his duty to bring them up to his plane of religious thought, and not to descend to their low grade in order to obtain their applause or to be considered in harmony with the "spirit of the age." Nor should he dignify with the misnomer of "Natural Religion" (as does the author of *Ecce Homo*) the thinly-veiled paganism of the worshippers of "culture" in this nineteenth century. Professor Seelye, in this his latest work, makes the following declaration : " Especially of late years and among ourselves art and science have proclaimed themselves to be not mere rebels against the reigning religion, but rival religions." This assuredly points to a new religion of *culture* that is, according to its votaries, to take the place of Christianity. It is sad to see such an able man as the author of *Ecce Homo*, and the president of a well-known American college, infected with the views of this neo-paganism. He boldly declares that "it is a mistake to imagine Christianity as standing or falling with the miracle of the Resurrection." "If we look, as Protestants are disposed to do, at the original institution of Christianity, we find it growing out of the single alleged fact of the Resurrection; we find St. Paul himself declaring that without that fact it is nothing—the fact being precisely one of those which the modern scientific school puts on one side. On the other hand, the Catholic view is still more pitilessly dogmatic."* Very true, professor, and more than likely to remain so—the same to-day, yesterday, and to-morrow, teach-

* *Natural Religion*, p. 216.

ing the unchangeable truths of God's revelation.

We are not, therefore, surprised to learn
from the recapitulation of his own work
that he "has not aimed at combating the
scepticism of the age. It has rather assumed that a system of doctrine which
has been left unrevised for more than a
thousand years must needs provoke scepticism."* He evidently thinks that there
is too much of the *supernatural* in the
Christian creed : "Supernatural religion, all
must feel, has not done so much, has not
reformed the world so much, as might
have been expected. Its failure is evidently due in great part to its supernaturalism, to the unnatural stress it lays upon
a future life."

Supernatural religion does not attempt

* Ibid. p. 234.

to coerce the free-will of man. Every individual is perfectly at liberty to follow its promptings or to throw obstacles in the way of its progress, and this is the only reason why the true Christian religion, or " supernatural religion," has not entirely reformed the world.

So this strange scientific school entirely rejects all faith in the supernatural ; and blind indeed must they be who do not clearly see that whatever of pure civilization this age possesses has all sprung from belief in the *supernatural* and the fair fruits it has produced over the face of the earth during its reign over the minds and hearts of men.

Mr. Mallock, who, whilst professing no religion, yet candidly admits that if we cast aside the supernatural we would necessarily take away the chief merit even from the greatest masterpieces of art and literature, before which these scientists bow in admiration, if not in worship, thus speaks: " Let us turn to the world's greatest works of art—I mean its dramas; for just as poetry is the most articulate of all the arts, so is the drama the most comprehensive form of poetry." Referring to the " Antigone" of Sophocles, the " Macbeth" and " Hamlet" of Shakspere, and the " Faust" of Goethe, he says : " What is the chief faculty in us that they appeal to? It will need but little thought to show us that they appeal primarily to the supernatural moral judgment; that this judgment is perpetually being expressed explicitly in the works themselves, and, which is far more important, that it is always presupposed in us. In other words, these supreme manifestations of life are presentations of men struggling or failing to struggle, not after natural happiness, but after supernatural right; and it is always presupposed on our part that we admit this struggle to be the one important thing. . . . It will be thus seen, and the more we consider the matter the more plain will it become to us, that in all such art as that which we have been now considering the premises on which all its power and greatness rests is this: The grand relation of man is not first to his brother-men, but to something else that is beyond humanity, that is at once without and beyond himself; to this first, and to his brother-men through this. We are not our own; we are bought with a price. Our bodies are God's temples, and the joy and terror of life depend on our keeping these temples pure or defiling them. Such are the solemn and profound beliefs, whether conscious or unconscious, on which all the higher art of the world has based itself." *

Eliminate the element of supernaturalism from religion and you take away its very essence, you sap the foundations of morality, resolve order into chaos, take away from human life its true value as well as its true meaning, and plunge us into worse than Egyptian darkness, shutting us out for ever from the rays of that most beneficent "Light that enlighteneth every man that cometh into the world."

But, thanks to the All-wise and All-powerful "Giver of every good and perfect gift," there is no danger that that Light shall ever be withdrawn from us, for it will always shine forth from the Citadel of the Lord, the House of the Living God,

* *Is Life Worth Living?* pp. 147–150.

"the pillar and ground of truth," against which not all the assaults of error, heresy, or infidelity, nor even those of hell itself, can ever prevail: "No weapon that is formed against thee shall prosper; and every tongue that resisteth thee in judgment thou shalt condemn."*   "For the nation and the kingdom that will not serve thee shall perish. . . . And the children of them that afflict thee shall come bowing down to thee, and all that slander thee shall worship the steps of thy feet, and shall call thee the City of the Lord, the Sion of the Holy One of Israel."†

CHURCH OF ST. JOHN THE EVANGELIST, SYRACUSE, N. Y.,
FEAST OF ST. JAMES THE APOSTLE, July 25, 1885.

* Isaias liv. 17.   † Ibid. lx. 12–14.

THE KEYS OF THE KINGDOM.

Is Religion worthy of Man's Study?

T is a clear sign of the strange spirit of the age when such a question is asked and submitted for examination. There is no reason why it should not be met and properly answered. For indifference is the crying evil of the times, and is but the natural consequence of the so-called liberality of the age in which we live. We are not of those, let it be borne in mind, who cry down the nineteenth century, and who believe it to be the very personification of evil, the very reign of Antichrist. There is much to admire in this age, and very much indeed for which we all owe our most heartfelt thanks to Almighty God, the Giver of every good and perfect gift. There is far more liberty than in former times, although here and there, especially in some European countries, there is the excess of liberty, or license. There has been much undoubted progress made in all human sciences, astounding discoveries, marvellous inventions, and vast improvements as to the material welfare of the individual considered in his comforts and the conveniences of life.

There is certainly no lack of liberality— and with that, when it is *genuine*, we have no wish to find fault—but we believe that even liberality can reach an extreme. Far be it from us to sigh over the ages that are past, or to wish to recall the era of religious persecution—the most hateful of all kinds of persecution; yet there was one treasure possessed by the people of the middle ages that all sincere, religiously-disposed persons might well desire to enjoy, even in this progressive age, and that is religious unity. Whatever may be the faults ascribed to those who lived in those old times, it must certainly be admitted that they had strong Christian faith and the magnificent enthusiasm which is born of it, that was willing to make any sacrifice for religion. They bequeathed to the generations that were to follow them imperishable marks of their devotion in those grand and imposing temples erected to God's honor, which are a source of admiring wonder to this cold, materialistic age.

There is a spirit of false liberality afloat

that infects the entire religious atmosphere. The so-called liberalist seems to have but one doctrine—namely, that he respects all religions and forms of religion, and that they are all equally good; but if you will really sound him to the very bottom you will find that he means that sensible men such as he, those fully abreast with the dominant spirit of the times, should not trouble themselves with religion in any shape or form, as it is something unworthy of serious study and attention. He may possibly admit, by a wonderful condescension, that it is an excellent thing for women and children, but decidedly beneath the consideration of men of nineteenth-century culture.

As there are not a few naturally good men and honorable citizens—especially in this great country of ours—who are unfortunately imbued with these sentiments and infected with the virulent poison of indifference, we deem it well to consider this question, " Is religion worthy of man's study ?" and to answer it by showing that there is no study in the world that can possibly be compared with it in importance, in true grandeur, in urgent necessity and unspeakable advantages.

The importance of a study is judged by the value of the end in view. The objects of the different human sciences—astronomy, geology, chemistry, mathematics, etc.—are limited, confined to the present life, its passing interests, pleasures, or conveniences. None of them, not even philosophy, can answer satisfactorily the most important questions that suggest themselves to every human mind. Philosophy, separated from religion, rejects all creeds and gives us nothing but opinions, more or less vague, on the most necessary objects of man's inquiry. No one has ever given us a better description of the wrangles of philosophers, and no one, perhaps, was more capable of judging them, than one of their own greatest leaders in modern times —Jean Jacques Rousseau. He thus describes his philosophic brethren :

" I have consulted our philosophers, I have perused their books, I have examined their several opinions; I have found them all proud, positive, and dogmatizing, even in their pretended scepticism, knowing everything, proving nothing, and ridiculing one another; and this is the only point in which they concur and in which they are right. Daring when they attack, they defend themselves without vigor. If you consider their arguments, they have none but for destruction; if you count their number, each one is reduced to himself; they never unite but to dispute; to listen to them was not the way to relieve myself from my doubts. I conceived that the insufficiency of the human understanding was the first cause of this prodigious diversity of sentiment, and that pride was the second. If our philosophers were able to discover truth, which of them would interest himself about it? Each of them knows that his system is not better established than the others, but he supports it because it is his own; there is not one amongst them who, coming to distinguish truth from falsehood, would not prefer his own error to the truth that is discovered by another. Where is the philosopher who, for his own glory, would not willingly deceive the whole human race? Where is he who, in the secret of his heart, proposes any other object than his own distinction? Provided he can but raise himself above the commonalty, provided he can eclipse his competitors, he has reached the summit of his ambition. The great thing for him is to think differently from other people. Among believers he is an atheist; among atheists he is a believer. Shun, shun then those who, under pretence of explaining nature, sow in the hearts of men the most dispiriting doctrines, whose scepticism is far more affirmative and dogmatical than the decided tone of their adversaries. Under pretence of being themselves the only people enlightened, they imperiously subject us to their magisterial decisions, and would fain palm upon us, for the true causes of things, the unintelligible systems they have erected in their own heads ; whilst they overturn, destroy, and trample under-foot all that mankind reveres, snatch from the afflicted the only comfort left them in their misery, from the rich and great the only curb that can restrain their passions, tear from the heart all remorse for vice, all hope of virtue, and still boast of themselves as the benefactors of mankind. 'Truth,' they say, 'is never hurtful to man.' I believe that as well as they ; and the same, in my opinion, is a proof that what *they* teach is not the truth."

What a true, vivid picture is here presented to us, though written in the last century, of the infidel philosophers and scientists of our day, who cannot agree among themselves, yet discard religion and "trample under-foot" all that mankind has ever held most dear and sacred ! Truly, it takes one of themselves to describe accurately their own peculiar features; and well indeed has the great French philosopher done it, in words that give forth no uncertain sound.

In these conferences we take it for granted that we are addressing men—men worthy of the name—who believe they have a soul and that that soul is immortal. Those who believe it not place themselves—there is no necessity for us to do it—on a level with the brute creation. Such men, having abdicated their reason and stifled its highest aspirations, cannot be reasoned with on such momentous questions, for there is no basis on which to work, no foundation on which to build.

"All men are vain," says the inspired writer (Wisdom xiii. 1), "in whom there is not the knowledge of God." How any man gifted with reason can behold the

earth with all its fruitfulness, the wonders
of the mineral, the vegetable, and the animal kingdoms, the incomparable beauty of
the firmament, the majestic order and undisturbed harmony of the stellar universe,
and possibly call into doubt the existence
of an All-wise and Almighty Creator, goes
beyond our comprehension. "The fool
hath said in his heart, There is no God"
(Psalm xiii. 1). Fénelon, the amiable and
holy Archbishop of Cambray, was one
evening walking with the young prince
whose preceptor he was, when the following incident—which we give in the words
of the late Mgr. de Ségur—took place:

"The heavens glittered with a thousand
stars. The horizon was still gilded by the
last rays of the setting sun. All nature
was at rest, beautiful and sublime. The
child asking what ·hour it was, the good

bishop drew out his watch. 'What a beautiful watch, monseigneur!' said his young pupil. 'Will you allow me to look at it?' The archbishop gave it to him, and as he was examining it closely Fénelon said: 'It is a very singular thing, my dear Louis, that that watch made itself.' 'Made itself!' repeated the child, looking at his master with a smile. 'Yes, entirely alone. A traveller found it in some desert, and it seems quite certain that it made itself.' 'That is impossible!' young Louis answered. 'Monseigneur is laughing at me.' 'No, my child, I am not laughing at you. What is there impossible in what I have said?' 'But, monseigneur, a watch could never make itself!' 'And why?' 'Because so much precision is needed in the arrangement of the thousand little wheels which cause its motion and make the hands keep time that it requires great intelligence to organize it; and even then very few men really succeed in the operation. That such an article could make itself is absolutely impossible; you have been deceived, monseigneur.'

" Fénelon embraced the child, and, pointing out to him the starlit heavens above their heads, he said : 'What will you think, then, dear Louis, of those who pretend that all the wondrous heavens have not only made themselves but preserve themselves in an unbroken order, and that there is no God?' 'Are there men so foolish and so wicked as to say that?' asked the boy. 'Yes, dear child, there are those who *say* it, few in number, thank God.' 'But are there any who believe it? I can scarcely credit that there are, considering how entirely they must do violence to their reason, their heart, their instinct, and their good sense before they can maintain such an opinion. If it be evident that a watch cannot make itself, is it not far more so of man himself, by whom watches are made? There was a *first* man, for all things have their beginning, and this beginning is universally attested by the history of the human race. It is certain, then, that some one made the first man. This some one is that Being who made all beings, who has Himself been made by no one, and whom we call God. He is infinite, for there is no limit to His being; He is eternal—that is to say, infinite in duration, without beginning and without end; almighty, just, good, holy, perfect, and infinite in all His perfections. He is everywhere and invisible, and no one can fathom His marvels. It is in

Him we live and move and have our being. He is our first principle and our last end.'"

Believing in God, therefore, and that He must necessarily be all-wise as well as all-powerful, we believe, likewise, that He has placed in us, in our inmost being, in our very soul, aspirations for immortality and an intimate consciousness that such is our destiny. Being infinitely good, He certainly would not create and implant in our bosoms hopes, desires, aspirations He never intended to satisfy. This has been the constant, invariable belief of all times and of all peoples,. and this fact furnishes in itself an infallible motive of certitude, aided most powerfully by that intimate sense or interior consciousness, the inalienable possession of every child of Adam, every member of the human race.

The words of Plato, the great pagan philosopher, ought to put to shame the infidels of our time.   Speaking on the immortality of the soul, he says :

" O my friends ! if the soul is really immortal what care should be taken of her, not only in respect of the portion of time which is called life, but eternity !   And the danger of neglecting her from this point of view does indeed appear to be awful.   If death had only been the end of all, the wicked would have had a good bargain in dying, for they would have been happily quit not only of their body but of their own evil together with their souls.   But now, inasmuch as the soul is manifestly immortal, there is no release or salvation from evil except the attainment of the highest virtue and wisdom.   For the soul, when on her progress to the world below, takes nothing with her but nurture and education; and these are said greatly to benefit or greatly to injure the departed at the very beginning of his pilgrimage in the other world." *

In his work on laws, addressing himself to young men, Plato speaks of "a divine justice which neither you nor any other unfortunate will ever glory in escaping, and which the ordaining powers have specially ordained; take good heed of them, for a day will come when they will take heed of you. If you say, I am small and will creep into the depths of the earth, or I am high and will fly up to heaven, you are not so small or so high but that you shall pay the fitting penalty, either in the world below or in some yet more savage place still, whither you shall be conveyed."

* *Phædo*, i. 437 (Jowett's translation).

In another part of the same work he says:
"Of all the things which a man has, next
to God, his soul is the most divine and
most truly his own. Now, in every man
there are two parts—the better and superior part which rules, and the worse and
inferior part which serves; and the ruler
is always to be preferred to the servant."

Raised above every other earthly creature by the gift of reason, made lord of
the inferior creation, endowed with an immortal soul, formed in the very image of
the Triune God, by the triple faculty of
will, memory, and understanding, we must
confess that that must be the most important of all sciences which alone can answer
the very first questions of our soul—the
superior part of our nature. These questions, which naturally suggest themselves
to every mind capable of reasoning, are:

" Whence do I come ?" " Why am I here ?" " Whither do I tend ?"

Religion is the only science that can effectually answer these all-important questions, and therefore is it most worthy of every man's study, of his earnest, constant, persevering attention. It points out to us our noble origin—that we came forth from God ; that our bodies, so wonderful in their organization, were formed, by His Almighty power, of the slime of the earth, but that our souls are the very breath, so to speak, of the Omnipotent—pure spirits that can never taste death. "God breathed into his nostrils the breath of life, and man became a living soul." .

What a satisfactory knowledge is this, and all the more so when it is contrasted with that very weak mental pabulum furnished us by some of the scientists of the present age, that we are the descendants of apes, who, in the course of ages, have developed into reasonable, civilized beings.

> "Thrice happy men,
> And sons of men, whom God hath thus advanced,
> Created in His image, there to dwell
> And worship Him, and in reward to rule
> Over His works, on earth, in sea, or air,
> And multiply a race of worshippers
> Holy and just! Thrice happy if they know
> Their happiness and persevere aright!"

Religion shows us whence we came, narrates the causes of our fall, demonstrates the need of redemption, imparts a faithful knowledge of the Saviour, constantly points out to us our grand, eternal destiny, and furnishes us with all the means necessary for its attainment. It alone gives us the key to the mysteries of life and shows us the hand of Divine Providence in the direction of the universe, in the rise and fall of nations and of empires. And, strange as it may appear to some, though chiefly intended to secure our happiness in the next life, it is the only power, the only influence, that can render us peaceful and content in this, that makes us satisfied with our state, that effectually helps us to bear not only with the inconveniences and discomforts, but chiefly with the misfortunes, attending our sojourn upon earth.

Even were we to ignore revelation, reason itself teaches us that man is such a superior being that nothing earthly can ever fully satisfy his longings and desires. Let him possess an abundance, and even a superabundance, of this world's goods, an indulgence full and complete of sensual pleasures, all the honors and all the glory that can be acquired in war or peace, the loftiest position that man can reach, the greatest success in invention, discovery, science, or art, and his soul will still continue unsatisfied. There will remain a certain undefined or undefinable restlessness, a seeking after something he has not as yet, a longing for something or some one far more perfect and entrancing, for "the eye is not filled with seeing, neither is the ear filled with hearing";* all of which goes to prove that he was created for a grander, nobler, holier destiny than can be obtained here below in this circumscribed earthly sphere.

No created love can ever fully satiate the cravings of the human heart, no knowledge nor science within man's reach or attainment can satisfy his intellect; for, being created for the contemplation and possession of Infinite Truth itself, all else would but serve to show how deep is the void which God alone can fill.

* Eccles. i. 8.

Wealth has no inherent power by which it can of itself produce any happiness, pleasure, or delight of any kind. It is not an *end* in itself, but only the means to an end. It may procure for us the pleasures, comforts, conveniences, and luxuries of life.

Pleasure itself is either sensual or intellectual. If merely sensual it only satisfies the lower part of our nature, in which we bear resemblance to the brute creation. Such pleasures, if unrestrained, only debase the mind and generate remorse, disgust, and innumerable evils of body and soul. If the pleasure be of an intellectual kind it does not entirely satiate, for the mind is constantly craving more and more knowledge, and whatever it has acquired is of its very nature limited and imperfect.

Neither can worldly glory nor worldly honors render man fully content, for ambition is as insatiable a passion as avarice. A most striking example of this was Alexander the Great, who, after having subjugated kingdom after kingdom to his sway, and caused the proudest monarchs to tremble at the very mention of his name, yet was inconsolable because there did not remain another world to conquer. There was indeed another world to conquer, far more important than any earthly conquest, but he knew not of it, or more probably cared nothing about it, for it was not to be won by the arms he was accustomed to wield. He was able to overcome the mightiest armies, but he was not able to conquer himself. "The patient man is better than the valiant, and he that ruleth his spirit than he that taketh cities." *

So we see that none of the chief ob-

* Proverbs xvi. 32.

jects for which men labor can ever fill the void in their souls, for the best of all reasons—that the Creator never intended that they should. Having made us for Himself, the contemplation of His eternal attributes and the participation of His own beatitude, we shall search the universe in vain for any object or any destiny other than the All-perfect Being Himself, who alone can fully answer our anxious longings and desires.

If the highest objects of earthly ambition do not and cannot completely satisfy their possessors, what can be said for the vast majority of the human race, who have never been, and in all probability never will be, in the enjoyment of wealth, honors, or distinction? If there were no hereafter to readjust the inequalities or to rectify the wrongs so plainly to be seen in the present life, what a miserable world this would be for most of the children of men! Take away religion and the magnificent hopes it holds out to the well-doer and to him who suffers in silence, then, most certainly, life would not be worth living to the countless millions who have to toil and suffer and bear the heavy burdens that crush them to the earth.

The All-powerful One, who, out of the promptings of an eternal love, brought us forth from nothingness, has not cast us into this world to perish miserably. To each one of His creatures, formed in His own divine likeness, He says: "I have loved thee with an everlasting love."* His providence watches, guides, and protects us. Even the very hairs of our head are numbered; and, no matter how lowly

* Jerem. xxxi. 3.

our condition, how bitter our sufferings,
how severe òur trials, we have the blessed
assurance that "to them that love God all
things work together unto good," * and
that "which is at present momentary and
light of our tribulation worketh for us
above measure exceedingly an eternal
weight of glory." † For Thou, O God!
"lovest all things that are, and hatest
none of the things which Thou hast made;
for Thou didst not appoint or make anything hating it. And how could anything
endure, if Thou wouldst not? or be preserved, if not called by Thee? But Thou
sparest all, because they are Thine, O
Lord! who lovest souls." ‡

Religion teaches us our chief business
in this world, that we are placed here
simply on probation, and that an eter-

* Rom. viii. 28.   † 2 Cor. iv. 17.   ‡ Wisdom xi. 25–27.

nity of happiness or an eternity of misery rests upon the issue. ˙ We are all endowed with free-will, and, as a necessary consequence, capable of merit or demerit. No man will be condemned for what he did not or could not know, or for actions for which he was not fully responsible. We are composed of body and spirit, and with body and spirit, therefore, we should worship our Creator. We should not only do what He commands and avoid what He forbids, but *believe* all that He proposes to our faith, and this entirely on the strength of His divine veracity, who can neither deceive nor be deceived. We must submit our *intellects* as well as our *wills* to God.

No man should decline the yoke of religion because of its mysteries. We are surrounded by mysteries even in the natural order. There are mysteries in and around us—mysteries that no philosopher or scientist, be they never so learned, can fathom or explain. Why, then, expect that in the higher order—the spiritual, the supernatural—there should not exist still more wonderful mysteries?

One of the most eminent philosophers and chemists of this age, the Swedish Professor Berzelius, confesses that, "with all the knowledge we possess of the forms of the body, considered as an instrument, and of the mixture and mutual bearings of the rudiments to one another, yet the cause of most of the phenomena within the animal body lies so deeply hidden from our view that it certainly never will be found. We call this hidden cause *vital power;* and, like many others who before us have in vain directed attention to this point, we make use of a *word* to which we can fix no idea. This *power to live* belongs not to the constituent parts of our bodies, nor does it belong to them as an instrument, neither is it a simple power, but the result of the mutual operation of the instruments on one another—a result which varies as the operations vary, and which often, from small changes and obstructions, ceases altogether. When our elementary books inform us that the vital power in one place produces from the blood the fibres of the muscle, in another a bone, in a third a medulla of the brain, and in another, again, certain humors which are destined to be carried off, we know after this explanation as little as we knew before. . . . Nothing of what chemistry has taught us hitherto has the smallest analogy to the operations of the nervous system, or affords us the least hint towards a knowledge of its occult nature; and the chain of our experience must *always* end in something inconceivable. Unfortunately, this *inconceivable something* acts the principal part in animal chemistry, and enters so into every process, even the most minute, that the highest knowledge which we can attain is the knowledge of the nature of the productions, whilst we are for ever excluded from the possibility of explaining how they are produced." *

There is no reason, then, to discard or to neglect the study of religion because it teaches many truths above our comprehension. We might as well cast aside human life on the same plea, for it, too,

* Brunmark's translation of Baron Berzelius' *View of the Progress and Present State of Animal Chemistry.*

has many secrets that are impenetrable. If we believe only in what is tangible or what falls under the perception of our senses, our horizon of knowledge must necessarily become very much narrowed and limited. As Paley remarks in his *Evidences of Christianity*, "the great powers of nature are all invisible. Gravitation, electricity, magnetism, though constantly present and constantly exerting their influence; though within us, near us, and about us; though diffused throughout all space, overspreading the surface or penetrating the contexture of all bodies with which we are acquainted, depend upon substances and actions which are totally concealed from our senses."

Apropos of this there is an amusing little incident told of the late Father Lacordaire, the eminent divine and orator of the Dominican Order. He was one Friday sitting at the *table-d'hôte* in a restaurant at Paris when a commercial traveller, who had made himself remarkable by his boisterous talk while trying to show himself a man of liberal ideas and entirely opposed to what he called superstition, in helping himself very plentifully to a dish of omelet passed the small remnants to the humble friar, and insolently remarked: "As for me, monsieur, I do not believe in anything I do not understand." "Ah! indeed," said the monk. "And will you have the kindness to tell me, apropos of the omelet that you are now eating, how is it that fire, which makes iron or lead soft and pliable, yet has the contrary effect on an egg by making it hard?"

"I confess I do not understand it, Monsieur l'Abbé." "Well, then," said the monk, "I see that your not understanding it does not prevent you from believing in omelets, as do likewise all the rest of the world."

We may rest assured that there was a good laugh at the expense of the commercial traveller, and that he was very silent during the rest of the meal.

Simple as this little incident may appear, it carries with it a lesson patent to all.

Religion alone explains—as far as can be explained—and certainly gives us all the knowledge as well as the means necessary to attain the end of our creation, and that is to love and serve God here in order that we may be happy with Him hereafter. Reaching that desirable end, all that is of any lasting value is thereby attained; failing to secure it, all that is of any lasting value is for ever lost. The mind of every man, of every earnest, right thinking man, does not fail to tell him in unmistakable accents that nothing on earth, whether in the shape of worldly science, riches, honors, or pleasures, can ever satiate the cravings of his mind for knowledge or the longings of his heart for love. He was made for God, and God alone, therefore, can adequately fill the void of the human soul and satisfy its aspirations.

The study of religion, then, is the most important of all studies. How sublime it is, how elevating in its character, purifying in its nature, deeply moral in tone, and incomparably grand in its range of objects! It raises man above himself, makes him forget the petty interests and miserable seekings of this earthly life, and causes him to soar aloft in the contemplation of eternal truth. It makes a man conscious of his true dignity, shows him the value of his immortal soul, invests him with a more exalted sense of his responsibility, and enables him to see the action of Divine Providence in all the events of life. Though not gifted with great talents or deep learning, though walking in the humbler paths of life, yet, by means of his religion and the contemplation of its mysteries, the humblest Christian can reach, even here below, a higher sphere of thought than the brightest and most philosophic minds that depend on their own resources.

Religion brings the clearest light to the mind, the greatest peace to the soul. It is the only power that can restrain from excess in prosperity, alleviate in distress, cheer in despondency, sweeten labor, lighten sorrow, banish envy and discontent, strengthen order, stabilitate government, and—far more important than all—bridge over the terrible chasm of the grave.

No human science whatever can compare with religion, either in the certainty or the sublimity of its great teachings. Whilst thus justly extolling this study, far be it from us to depreciate any human science. Every science is good in itself and has a laudable end in view. When properly cultivated and earnestly pursued they most admirably show forth the wisdom and power of God in every department of nature: "Cœli enarrant gloriam Dei, et opera ejus firmamentum"—The heavens declare the glory of God, and the firmament His works.

Science and religion should go hand-in-hand. Human science and philosophy are the handmaids of religion, and religion blesses their efforts and crowns their labors. Many of the scientists and philosophers of the present age have striven with all their might to divorce science from religion; but they should not, and, in fact, never can, be divorced. There is no antagonism between them. It is absolutely impossible that there should be. God is the author of the natural as well as of the supernatural order; and if there were any such opposition between the truths of one order and the truths of another, God would be contradicting Himself. Such an idea is absolutely repugnant to the infinite wisdom of God. The more human sciences become perfected and the more fully they attain their legitimate end, the more will the great truths of revelation be made evident to the world and shine with greater brilliancy. Then will all apparent contradictions and seeming opposition fade away and give place to the light of eternal truth. The Catholic Church in her last Œcumenical Council of the Vatican, when treating of the necessarily harmonious relations existing between reason and revelation, thus speaks of her attitude towards human science: "Far be it from the Church to hamper the cultivation of human arts and sciences; she, on the contrary, comes to their aid and assists them in many ways. For neither does she ignore nor despise the advantages to life they bring in their train; rather does she confess that the sciences, coming as they do from God, the Lord of all science, if they be treated with the proper spirit—by means of God's grace—lead the mind back to Him." *

As Lord Bacon said, a little knowledge leadeth away from God, but more know-

* Conc. Vatic., cap. iv. De Fide et Ratione.

ledge bringeth one back again. The Catholic Church condemns only false science— the knowledge, based on false principles, that serves but to lead men astray from their true and high destiny. Hence she has justly condemned the following proposition : " Human reason is, without any regard to God, the only true arbiter of true and false, of good and evil ; it is its own law, it suffices by its natural powers to secure the happiness of men and of nations." *
In the words of our illustrious Pontiff, Leo XIII., shortly before ascending the throne of Peter, the Catholic Church cannot look with favor on " that science which dives into matter and assigns it to eternity, that goes up to the firmament and descends into the bowels of the earth to look in vain for an argument with which

* Syllabus.

to destroy Biblical cosmogony; that science which debases man to the level of the brute, and which, by its extravagances, shakes the very foundations of moral, domestic, and civil order, the Church cannot but oppose. Now, every man knows that, far from complaining, he ought to raise his hands to God in thanksgiving for having sent into this world that Infallible Authority which, while it invokes every blessing for the present and for the future, likewise preserves every blessing for us by rescuing us from the impious hands of those who would snatch them from our grasp."*

In this same most admirable pastoral letter—written by the same skilful hand that holds so firmly, yet so gently, the helm of Peter's Bark—we find this strong and beautiful passage: "If the Church is

* Cardinal Pecci's Pastoral Letter for 1877.

alarmed at the ruin that a few vain men can make, who imagine they understand everything because they have a slight smattering of many things, she has every confidence in those who devote their minds to the deep and serious study of nature, because she knows that at the end of their researches they will find God, who displays Himself in His works with all the unimpeachable attributes of His power, wisdom, and goodness. If some learned sage, in studying nature, goes away from God, it is a sign that the heart of the unfortunate man is already contaminated by the venom of infidelity that has entered into him through the avenue of culpable passions. He did not become an atheist because he cultivated learning, which should naturally develop far nobler results. Indeed, the large majority of those who acquire great and lasting knowledge in the sciences through the studies they have gone through and by their ingenious discoveries, have, as it were, erected a ladder with which to mount to heaven and glorify God."

"The great astronomer Copernicus was profoundly religious. Kepler, another father of modern astronomy, thanked God for the pleasure He made him experience in his ecstasies, in which he was transported by the contemplation of the works of His hands. Galileo, to whom experimental philosophy is indebted for so powerful an impetus, was led, by his studies, to declare that the Holy Scriptures and nature alike point out the works of God: the first as dictated by the Holy Spirit, the second as the faithful performer of His laws.

" Linnæus, by his study of nature, was so inflamed that the words which dropped from his lips were like those of a psalm: 'God eternal,' he exclaimed, 'Immense, Omniscient, Omnipotent! Thou hast appeared to me, in some manner, in the works of creation, and I have been overwhelmed with wonder. In all the works of Thy hand, even the smallest and most insignificant, what power, what wisdom, and what unspeakable perfection do I behold! . . . Fontenelle, who, it appears, was regarded as the encyclopædia of his time in the France of the eighteenth century, already poisoned by the breath of infidelity, could not help saying: 'The importance of the study of physics does not proceed so much from the fact that it satisfies our curiosity, but because it lifts us up to a less imperfect knowledge of the Author of the universe, and revives in our minds the sentiments of veneration and admiration which we owe Him.' Alexander Volta, the immortal inventor of the voltaic battery, was a sincere Catholic, and, in times that were not propitious to faith, gloried in being a Catholic and did not blush at the Gospel. Faraday, the illustrious chemist, saw a means by which to reach God in the science he was passionately studying, and he could not tolerate infidels." *

The names of others no less distinguished in science, and who at the same time were strong believers in Christianity, might easily be brought forward in no small number, but we shall only mention a few: Sir Isaac Newton, the great astronomer and mathematician; Hugh Mil-

* N. Y. *Freeman's Journal's* translation.

ler and Sir Roderick Murchison, geologists ; Sir Humphry Davy, George Stephenson, and last, though not least, Father Secchi, of the Roman Observatory. One of the most interesting and important meetings of scientific men that ever assembled was that of the British Association in 1865, when a declaration, drawn up and signed by six hundred and seventeen of its members—many of whom hold the highest rank and influence in scientific circles—was given to the world, solemnly professing their belief in the inspiration of the Bible and the absence of any incompatibility between its utterances and the conclusions of science. Their resolutions are well worthy of perusal and meditation :

" We, the undersigned students of the natural sciences, desire to express our sincere regret that researches into scientific truth are perverted by some in our own times into occasions for casting doubt upon the truth and authenticity of the Holy Scriptures.

"We conceive that it is impossible for the word of God as written in the book of Nature, and God's word written in Holy Scripture, to contradict each other, however much they may appear to differ.

"We are not forgetful that physical science is not complete, but is only in a condition of progress, and that at present our finite reason enables us only to see as through a glass darkly, and we confidently believe that a time will come when the two records will be seen to agree in every particular.

"We cannot but deplore that natural science should be looked upon with suspicion by many who do not make a study of it, merely on account of the unadvised manner in which some are placing it in opposition to Holy Writ.

"We believe that it is the duty of every scientific student to investigate nature simply for the purpose of elucidating truth, and that if he finds that some of his results appear to be in contradiction to the written Word, or rather to his own interpretations of it, which may be erroneous, he should not presumptuously affirm that his own conclusions must be right and the statements of Scripture wrong. Rather leave the two side by side till it shall please God to allow us to see the manner in which they may be reconciled ; and instead of insisting upon the seeming differences between science and the Scriptures, it would be as well to rest in faith upon the points in which they agree."

This is the true spirit in which to engage in studies of this nature, and it was a noble declaration for Christian scientists to make in the face of this scientific nineteenth century. Dr. Samuel Kins, F.R.A.S., in his very able and deeply interesting work, *The Harmony of the Bible with Science*, gives the entire list of names of the signers of this declaration, among which we notice such distinguished men as Sir David Brewster, Sir J. R. Bennett, M.D., the Balfours, Abercrombies, Andersons, Bosworth, Fraser, Gibb, De La Harp, Dr. McLeod, Sir Charles Reed, and Sir John Richardson, M.D., LL.D., members of the leading scientific associations of Europe.

This study, then, is not only grand and sublime, but also most indispensable. It is the "unum necessarium"—the one thing necessary for us all. We can attain our true destiny without the study of astronomy or of foreign languages, mathematics, geology, or philosophy; but it is impossible without the knowledge of religion. It is a science within reach of all. It does not require great talents or broad education. The means are always at hand for its attainment. No one is debarred from the undertaking. The poor as well as the rich, the illiterate as well as the learned, the simple-minded as well as the philosopher, can drink at the same fountain of eternal truth. All that is required is simply good-will, earnestness, application. Ignorance of religion is, then, a crime when there are so many means within reach for obtaining the necessary knowledge. Indifference with regard to it is an outrage against the Almighty, an insult to Christ, a mark of contempt for His labors, His sufferings, His commands, His warnings: "He that believeth not shall be condemned."

Some form of religion, then, should be embraced, but only one can be true. "One Lord, one faith, one baptism." No man is free to choose his own way or to make his own creed, otherwise there were no need for Christ to come upon earth, if men could save their souls without His aid.

Coming as He did, it was undoubtedly to point out the way, the only sure one; and in that path, narrow as it may seem, every one is obliged to walk, otherwise he is on the wrong road, the broad one leading to destruction, and many there are who go by the same.

Now, as to what is the way, which is

the path, what is the rule of faith laid down by Christ and which we are all bound to follow, we hope to be able to explain in the following chapter.

What Rule of Faith was laid down by Christ?

THE creature owes to his Creator the worship of his whole being. He should adore Him with all the powers of his body and with all the faculties of his mind. He should bow down not only his will in obedience to the Lord's commands, but also his intellect to whatever He proposes to our belief. There are some very lofty and important truths within the reach of human reason—such as, for instance, the existence of a Supreme, Eternal Being who is the First Cause, the providence of God, and the immortality of the soul. It stands to reason, likewise, that there are, and must necessarily be, many truths above our comprehension and beyond the reach of our intellect and its limited capabilities. There are many truths, therefore, known to God and not known to men, and these He can most certainly communicate in the manner and in the measure He deems fit. There is no repugnance, then, in the idea of revelation; certainly none on the part of God, who as God is omniscient, and consequently no truth can be hidden or unknown to Him; and who is omnipotent as well as omniscient, and therefore innumerable means are at His command for making known these truths to mankind.

There is no repugnance to revelation on the part of man, for, being gifted with reason and intelligence, his mind has been formed for the reception of truth and the consequent increase of knowledge. Nor can there be any repugnance arising from the truths themselves: for though they may transcend the natural power of the intellect, yet they can be received, entertained, and believed on the authority of God Himself, resting, as they do, upon His divine veracity.

In the beginning man was gifted with a sublime knowledge of the truth. There was then no disorder in his intellect, no weakness in his will. His mind undeviatingly sought *the true*, his will *the good*. But when he sinned, seeking too curiously that knowledge which was forbidden him, sin and evil entered and cast a cloud upon his intellect, warped his judgment, weakened his once powerful will, and depraved his affections. Man then gradually pursued a downward course. For a considerable time he preserved the principles of natural religion and adhered to patriarchal traditions ; but these, too, in time became clouded or corrupted, so that even the knowledge of the one true God would have been lost to the world if Divine Providence had not selected one race or people and made them the depository of His truth.

The Jewish people then alone excepted, all nations of the earth lived estranged from God, plunged in idolatry and following their own blind passions : " And as they liked not to have God in their knowledge, God delivered them up to a reprobate sense, to do those things which are not convenient, being filled with all iniquity, malice, fornication, covetousness, wickedness, full of envy, murder, conten-

tion, deceit, malignity, whisperers, detrac-
tors, hateful to God, contumelious, proud,
haughty, inventors of evil things, disobedient to parents, foolish, dissolute, without affection, without fidelity, without
mercy. Who, having known the justice
of God, did not understand that they who
do such things are worthy of death : and
not only they who do them, but they
also who consent to them that do them." *

From this terrible arraignment of pagan
society by the great Apostle St. Paul
we can easily see that corruption was on
the increase up to the very dawn of the
Christian era. Neither philosophy nor
literature and the arts were able to stem
the fearful tide. If the highest culture
that mankind ever reached, leaving God
and His knowledge aside, could have pre-

* Epistle to the Romans i. 28–32.

vented the grossest immorality. Greece and Rome would have been successful in attaining this result ; but the more they advanced in mere material civilization the deeper did they become immersed in the basest sensuality and the most barbarous inhumanity. Rome, the proud mistress of the earth, was noted, as Canon Farrar remarks, for "its enormous wealth, its unbounded self-indulgence, its coarse and tasteless luxury, its greedy avarice, its sense of insecurity and terror, its apathy, debauchery, and cruelty, its hopeless fatalism, its unspeakable sadness and weariness, its strange extravagances alike of infidelity and superstition." * The races of men strove long and obstinately to live without God, and they found only misery and despair.

*The Early Days of Christianity. p. 2.

The fulness of time had come and God stooped in loving mercy to fallen man. It became necessary for Him to manifest Himself and His divine truth to the human race, otherwise all hope would have perished for ever.   The Eternal Father, out of love for those whom He created in the image of the Godhead, sent His own Beloved Son, the Second Person of the ever-adorable Trinity, to earth to be clothed with our humanity, in order that "in the likeness of our sinful flesh" He might draw near to us and draw us nearer to Him, teach us "the way, the truth, the life," and lay down His life for us that we might have life more abundantly.

Hence Christ, the "true light which enlighteneth every man that cometh into this world," came upon earth to enlighten us, to teach us the great mysteries of religion, to point out the only true way to salvation and eternal happiness. Having come to show us the way, which the vast majority of men had totally lost sight of through the darkness of paganism, the mists of error, and the oppressive atmosphere of prejudice and passion, it would be the height of folly as well as of ingratitude to refuse to walk in the path thus pointed out, or to presume to select one for one's self other than that mapped out so clearly by Infinite Wisdom Incarnate.

"Wishing all men," without distinction of race or color or station in life, "to be saved and to arrive at the knowledge of truth," as the Sacred Scriptures declare, this wish cannot be a vain or illusory one on the part of God. Therefore He must certainly place within man's reach the means necessary for attaining this desirable end. Coming, as He did, to point out the way, that way ought to be a clear way, a sure way, a way open to all and within reach of the illiterate as well as the learned, the poor as well as the rich, the simple-minded as well as the philosopher (for the soul of the one is as precious in His sight as the soul of the other), and a way adapted to every clime, to every age, and to every disposition: "This shall be unto you a straight way, so that fools shall not err therein."*

Christ's stay upon earth was to be short, and the time devoted to His public mission was to be still shorter—only three years out of the thirty-three of His mortal life—yet He accomplished the great

* Isaias xxxv. 8.

objects for which He left His heavenly home. He came to offer Himself a willing Victim for the sins of men, and to establish a Church which was to be the depository of the infinite merits acquired by His labors, sufferings, and death, and the depository likewise of all the teachings He wished to inculcate in the minds of men. Before departing from earth He selected His Apostles to continue the work which He so gloriously began. To accomplish this grandest of missions He endowed them with His own divine authority. The same commission He received from His Heavenly Father He gave unto them : "As the Father hath sent Me, I also send you."* "All power is given to Me in heaven and on earth," He declares, and by virtue of that power

* St. John xx. 21.

He sends them forth in His own name to bear His message unto all men: "Go ye, therefore, and teach all nations; baptizing them in the name of the Father, and of the Son, and of the Holy Ghost, teaching them to observe all things whatsoever I have commanded you." And as this divine mission was not to end with their lives, but was to continue during all time through the ministry of their official successors, He solemnly declares: "And behold, I am with you all days, even to the consummation of the world." *

Thus did Christ appoint a body of teachers for His Church—a body of teachers that was never to fail, "the ministers of Christ and the dispensers of the mysteries of God" † unto all generations. To secure their union for evermore,

* St. Matt. xxviii. 18-20.   † 1 Cor. iv. 1.

to prevent all schisms and heresies from
rending His Church, He appointed the
Blessed Peter (and in him his successors)
the centre of authority, the immovable
rock on which He built His Church:
" Thou art Peter [or a rock]; and on this
rock I will build my Church, and the
gates of hell shall not prevail against it.
And I will give to thee the keys of the
kingdom of heaven. And whatsoever thou
shalt bind upon earth, it shall be bound
also in heaven ; and whatsoever thou shalt
loose upon earth, it shall be loosed also in
heaven." *

This Church, then, built upon St. Peter
—the " rock "—our Saviour made the depository of His infinite merits, of all His
teaching and all His power. He thus
founded a living teaching authority which

* St. Matt. xvi. 18, 19.

was to speak to all men in His name, to be for ever under His own most special protection, to withstand all the assaults of hell, and to be preserved from all false teaching by the perpetual, unfailing guidance of the Holy Spirit : " And I will ask the Father, and He shall give you another Paraclete, that He may abide with you for ever: the Spirit of Truth, whom the world cannot receive." *   " But the Paraclete, the Holy Ghost, whom the Father will send in My name, He will teach you all things, and bring all things to your mind, whatsoever I shall have said to you." †

This teaching authority of the Church which is to last for all time and to be for ever guided by the Spirit of Truth all men are obliged to hear and heed as they would Christ Himself : " He that heareth

* St. John xiv. 16, 17.   † Id. 26.

you heareth Me; and he that despiseth you despiseth Me; and he that despiseth Me despiseth Him that sent Me."* This declaration is plain, powerful, authoritative. This living voice of the Church, then, is to be heard by all; this is the rule of faith to be accepted by all, in every age, in every clime, no matter how brilliant their talents, how deep their learning, how lofty their position, how unbending their pride, or how strong their passions. The voice of the Church is, therefore, the voice of God, and its authority can never fail, for it rests upon the veracity of the Incarnate God, who has solemnly promised to abide with it for ever and to shield it against all the assaults of earth and hell. "Heaven and earth shall pass away before My words

* St. Luke x. 16.

shall fail." If the Catholic Church could be proved to have at any time failed as the teacher and guide of men, if it ever taught error or heresy or held up a false standard of morality, then Christ Himself would have failed in His promises, and Christianity as a divine system would fall to the ground, the greatest and saddest wreck in the universe. So plain and clear are those promises that they leave no chance of escape out of this dilemma— namely, either Christ was able to fulfil His promises or He was not. If able, as all who hold to His divine mission must necessarily believe, then the Catholic Church has never deviated for a moment from the true faith in the past, and never can deviate from it in the future. If not able to do what He so solemnly declared, then He was not what He represented

Himself to be, and merits not our love or trust. This is the reason why men of education who, unfortunately for themselves, lose the faith and abandon the Catholic Church, sink at once into infidelity. There is no half-way house for them; they are logical enough to see that there is no solid standing-ground between full Catholic faith and agnosticism, atheism, or infidelity, which practically are one and the same thing. When they fail to cling to the Rock of Peter there is no plank of safety whereon to lay hold amid the engulfing waves of error and heresy. Hence the Catholic Rule of Faith, the living, infallible voice of the Church, speaking to all ages and generations of men in the name of Christ Himself, perpetually assisted and protected by Him and guided by His Holy Spirit, is the only true, clear, and sure rule by following which men are to be saved.

Our separated brethren, however, declare that the Bible, and the *Bible only*, is the sure rule of faith; so let us examine calmly and see if this claim have any foundation on which it may rest and satisfy the just and natural requirements of the human mind.

Any one who has carefully and without prejudice read the history of the Catholic Church and who knows aught of its constant practice need not be told how much she has always venerated the Bible, how jealously she guarded it for hundreds of years in her own maternal bosom, how frequently she shielded it from the ravages of pagans, barbarians, and heretics, and handed it down pure and intact to the countless generations that were to follow.

It would be well for those outside the fold to bear in mind the undeniable fact that were it not for the Catholic Church *the Bible would not be now in existence;* that it was she who preserved most faithfully and gathered together the various parts of this Divine Book; that she cherished it and guarded it as her greatest treasure during all these long ages, and saved it from desecration as well as mutilation at the hands of its enemies; and that, in fine, holding it up to loving reverence, she makes it tend towards the spiritual progress, the eternal salvation and sanctification, of her countless members.

For nigh fifteen hundred years the Bible was in the sole possession of the Catholic Church, which handed it down to succeeding ages pure and intact; and yet Luther and his followers claim it as their own peculiar property. And how, I may justly ask, can any one outside of our holy religion, rejecting its authority and thus severing himself from that unbroken chain which, extending through so many ages of Catholic faith, connects the true members of God's Church of our day with Christ and His apostles—how, I ask, can such a one even prove that *there is* a Bible, that it is really authentic, canonical, and divinely inspired in all its parts? It is impossible, absolutely impossible, without recurring to that very same authority which he so contemptuously rejects and heartily despises. Appeal has to be made to that tradition which has been faithfully preserved in the Catholic Church from the first ages of the Christian era. But heretics do not acknowledge tradition, therefore no proof remains to them whereby to establish conclusively the authenticity, veracity, and canonicity of the Scriptures. The Bible itself does not declare the canonicity and inspiration of the various parts by which it is constituted, and it is beyond all doubt, to any one sufficiently acquainted with the ecclesiastical history of the first ages of Christianity, that some of the Scriptural writings now regarded as authentic were for a considerable time considered by many really doubtful until their canonicity was defined by Church authority. On what authority do Protestants accept one book as divinely inspired and reject another as uninspired? Why not accept the writings of St. Barnabas as well as those of St. Paul? They were both companions and apostolic missionaries, and certainly there are many beautiful and holy sentiments to be found in the epistle attributed to St. Barnabas. It was not received by the Council of Nice, and, therefore, those who reject it do so simply on the authority of the Church Catholic.

But, after all, how can he who rejects the claims of this same holy Church, "the pillar and ground of truth," to his submission and obedience; who believes that it was buried in ignorance, error, and corruption, and that it "fell away from the true faith of Christ"—how can he trust that same Church as to the preservation of the Scriptures? Would it not be very reasonable and very natural to suppose, under such an hypothesis, that this same Church, thus deserted by the grace of God and the indwelling light of the Holy Spirit, had changed the original text and corrupted the word of God? What surety, then, can such a one have that he really and truly possesses the Scriptures, such as they were given by the apostles and evangelists? None, absolutely none!

If the Church were the enemy, as it is declared, of the Bible, how can we explain the fact that for fifteen hundred years she preserved that work which is supposed to be an evidence of her own falling away from the true Gospel—an evidence of her own corruption in doctrines and morals? She would certainly have been wanting in worldly wisdom and worldly policy—a lack from which her enemies do not suppose her to suffer—thus laboriously to preserve the instrument of her own assumed destruction.

And what difficulties did she not have to surmount in order to preserve that holy work during so many ages! The art of printing was unknown until the middle of the fifteenth century. A book, especially one so voluminous as the Bible, took a great amount of time, labor, and anxiety to copy, and, when copied, a still greater solicitude and watchfulness in order to preserve it from the jealous hand of paganism and the ignorance of the barbaric hordes. Many a noble and heroic Christian suffered himself to be tortured, and even led to death, sooner than surrender those holy books which he prized dearer than life itself. Let us not forget the glorious examples and sacred memories of a St. Felix and a St. Eutropius, who underwent inexpressible pain and torture, and even a cruel death, rather than deliver up the Holy Scriptures into the hands of the persecutors of their faith.

Many are apt to lose sight of such models; and they who accuse our Holy Church of being inimical to the Word of God ought conscientiously to consider how much she reverences those who laid down their lives in order to preserve unto an ungrateful posterity that same volume which is *most abused* by those who *profess to use it most.*

The possession of a copy of the Bible in the middle ages, even up to the time in which Gutenburg flourished—the possession of such a work (in manuscript, of course, as it had to be) was considered a treasure. At least a year's labor of an exact penman was required to make a correct copy of the Holy Book.

The Venerable Bede tells us that even from his seventh year he devoted no inconsiderable part of his time to the meditation of the Scriptures. It was the chief exercise in which the monks and ecclesiastics of old took a holy delight and willingly expended their time and labor.

Poets drew their inspiration from the sacred pages, statesmen their great principles of law, painters and sculptors the grand subjects of their noblest efforts.

The great mass of the people could not read; and even if they were so capable, they could not procure, without the greatest difficulty and expense, a copy of any remarkable work, especially such a one as the Bible. They were not, however, deprived of its holy and salutary instructions, for everything seemed to speak to them in living expressions of Scripture. Their pastors explained to them the Divine Word; the altar and Holy Sacrifice recalled to their minds the life and death of their adorable Saviour; the life-like marble, the glowing canvas, embellished by artists never equalled in more modern times—all, all breathed forth the spirit and imaged the reality, beauty, and splendor of the divine writings.

We shall now consider the light in which the Catholic Church views the Bible, and inquire into the direct aim of the inspired writers in its composition.

In the first place, the Church does not acknowledge that there ever was a law given by Christ or His apostles, and she herself never promulgated one, decreeing that all the faithful, indiscriminately, should read the Bible. Never was any precept given to that effect, nor did there ever exist any real necessity for such a regulation.

Our Divine Redeemer, in founding our holy religion, proclaimed, by His own sacred lips, the saintly doctrines which He came upon earth to inculcate, and everywhere announced by word of mouth the great truths of His Gospel. He wrote nothing Himself, nor did He command anything to be written. He gave oral instructions to His apostles and disciples, and commanded them to do as He had done, and to go forth and *teach* all nations whatsoever they had learned from Him.

Conformably to the desires of their Master, they went forth and spread the truths of faith in every land, and communicated the light of the Gospel unto every people. They established almost numberless churches by their preaching and example, and had not recourse to *books* for the diffusion of Christianity.

In no part of the Scriptures can there be found a precept commanding their universal perusal. If Christ or His apostles had so wished, He or they would certainly have declared it; but this they have not done, as tradition testifies, and no proof can be brought forward to the contrary.

True it is that our Saviour says, "Search the Scriptures," or, according to the more proper version, and that sustained by the eminent Cardinal Wiseman and the distinguished Protestant bishop, Dr. Jebb, of Limerick, "You search the Scriptures," which, therefore, is to be taken in the *indicative* and not the *imperative* mood. This was not addressed to His disciples, but to the Scribes and Pharisees, who denied His mission and divinity, and whom He consequently referred to the inspired writings, principally those of Moses and the prophets, who, as He declared, gave testimony of Him.   He certainly did not refer to the New Testament, for at the time He spoke no such work existed.

Had our Blessed Saviour intended that

the Bible should be the only rule of faith and the exclusive means of salvation, He would certainly have devised some means whereby that sacred book could have been placed in the hands of all, since it was, under the supposition, absolutely necessary *for all.* In that case He undoubtedly would not have had the discovery of the art of printing delayed until nearly fourteen hundred years afterwards.

Moreover, if ever there did exist any obligation or indispensable necessity for the universal reading of the Bible, it should certainly have been in force particularly in the beginning of the Christian era, when nations were to be brought into the fold and various churches established. But most of the Christian churches were founded by the apostles and their immediate successors, by the preaching of the Word, and without the diffusion of books of Scripture. St. Irenæus, who lived at no very distant time from the apostles, and who flourished in the second century, declares that "the barbarous nations learned the faith without the aid of letters"—"*Gentes barbaræ sine litteris fidem didicerunt.*"

As St. Matthew's Gospel was not written until six years after the Ascension of our Lord, and St. John's Gospel not until sixty-three years afterwards, thousands, therefore, were received into the Church before one word of the New Testament was written, three thousand having been converted by the first sermon of St. Peter, as we may see by the second chapter of the Acts of the Apostles. Many thousands were received before St. John's Gospel was written, millions before all the inspired writings were gathered together and formed into one volume, and whole nations and hundreds of millions before the discovery of the art of printing. How, then, were all these generations of men to learn the truths of religion, if the Bible were the only rule of faith? Surely it would have been impossible. It would not only be unreasonable to expect it, but also contrary to all our ideas of the goodness of God and the infinite mercy of Christ, who wishes "all men to be saved and to arrive at the knowledge of truth."

Our Blessed Saviour did not say to His apostles, Go, write the New Testament, discover the art of printing, and *hand the Bible to every creature;* but "Go, teach all nations"; "Go ye into the whole world and *preach the Gospel* to every creature. He that believeth and is baptized shall be saved; but he that believeth not shall be condemned"—or, as the Protestant version expresses it, "shall be damned."*

" How, then, shall they call on him," says St. Paul, "in whom they have not believed? Or how shall they believe Him of whom they have not heard? And how shall they hear without a preacher? And how can they preach unless they be sent? As it is written : " How beautiful are the feet of them that preach the Gospel of peace, of them that bring glad tidings of good things! But all do not obey the Gospel. For Isaias saith : Lord, who hath believed our report? *Faith, then, cometh by hearing*, and hearing by the Word of Christ. But I say : Have they not heard? Yea, verily, their sound went over all the earth, and their words unto the ends of the whole world."†

* St. Mark xvi. 15, 16.   † Romans x. 14–19.

It is certain that the Holy Scriptures contain most of the great truths and dogmas of religion; but unassisted by the traditions of the early Church, which give to us the substance of the oral instructions of Christ and His apostles, as well as the meaning of the forms of language then in use—unassisted by these traditions and unsustained by the living, infallible authority in the Church, the Bible, of itself, would be insufficient for the formation of a religious people perfectly united and possessing the same invariable tenets, entirely agreeing in all important points of doctrine.

How difficult is the understanding of the Bible; how far above our comprehension, and above the reach of our reason and intellect, are many of its teachings and mysteries!

Who can fully understand that divinely-inspired work, whose history spreads over such an immense space of time, whose authors lived at such long intervals from one another, writing in various tongues, residing in different localities, possessing different characters and dispositions, and yet all being instruments in the hands of God for the diffusion of His Divine Word—that Divine Book, remarkable for its grandeur and at the same time its simplicity; now relating the most wonderful prodigies, and then recounting the most ordinary and apparently insignificant events; bringing us back to the creation of the world, into the garden of delights; pointing out to us our noble origin, mourning over our fall; leading us from the knowledge of patriarchal life to that of the mysterious wanderings of the chosen race and the miraculous events of the covenant established by God with His people—who would dare say that he can comprehend the wonderful depth and science of that book, so full of divine secrets, the most lofty truths, the most hidden mysteries, sufficient to baffle the greatest human skill, genius, and knowledge, and to confound the pride of the wisest on earth?

How many years of study and labor, joined with the most fervent and frequent prayer, did not the Fathers and Doctors of the Church spend in the meditation and interpretation of the Sacred Scriptures! And yet, with all their learning and wisdom, with all the aid they received from Heaven and all the help that human science could afford them, they knew and they felt that there were many depths not yet sounded, many mysterious passages not yet explored, and many secrets not yet disclosed to their investigating and inquiring glance.

By some strange contradiction, however, in human nature, how many there are who delude themselves with the idea that they can fully comprehend that mysterious book! They all admit the necessity of an instructor in every other branch of science; but "the science of the Scriptures," says the great St. Jerome, "is the only one which all persons indiscriminately claim as their own. This the babbling old woman, this the doting old man, this the wordy sophist take upon themselves, tear to tatters, teach before they themselves have learned." *

The Fathers and Doctors of the Church from the very beginning of her existence

* Epist. liii. ad Paulinam.

admitted that the Bible was a study, the immense depth of which could never be sufficiently fathomed. They loved and revered it, and many a lesson of wisdom and virtue they drew from its holy pages for their own instruction and sanctification, as well as for the edification and enlightenment of those entrusted to their care. They did not look upon it, however, as a complete and perfect rule of faith, as one containing all things necessary to be known and be believed, and as one from which each individual was to form his creed. They possessed another light, which they acknowledged as coming likewise from the Source of all light, and that is divine tradition, preserved inviolate and handed down to us from the time of Christ and His apostles. It is by this sacred light and the decision of the infallible Church that we believe the Bible to be divinely inspired in all its parts. As Lacordaire, the great French orator, declared: "Tradition is everywhere the mother of religion; it precedes and engenders sacred books, as language precedes and engenders scripture; its existence is rendered immovable in the sacred books, as the existence of the Word is rendered immovable in Scripture. A sacred book is a religious tradition which has had strength enough to sign its name."

The Bible teaches us many truths, but not all truth, as it was never so intended. Many outside the fold of the Church believe doctrines for which they will look in vain for proof in the Sacred Scriptures. They cannot, for instance, prove from the Bible the authenticity or inspiration of its various parts, nor why they worship on

Sunday, the first day of the week, rather than on the seventh, or Sabbath day.

If we consider the age in which we live, when copies of the Scriptures are spread over the world with the greatest profusion, and education, superficial though it be, is generally diffused, how many hundreds and thousands, ay, millions, there are who are not able to read, and who, if they were, could not understand the sacred writings !

How is it possible, then, to admit the proposition that an omnipotent God, so rich in mercy and goodness, in kindness and divine charity, should have appointed as the only means of salvation, as the only rule of faith, *one* so much above the capacity of the greater number of those for whom it was intended ? Is this the Gospel which Christ said He came on earth to preach to the poor ? Is *this* the prophecy of Isaias which He so earnestly declared He came to fulfil?

No, my friends, Christ never demands anything impossible of the human race. Wishing "*all men to be saved, and to arrive at the knowledge of truth,*" as He Himself so forcibly declared by word and deed, He placed means at their disposal within the reach and capacity of all. For that purpose He established His holy Church, which He enlightened and never ceases to enlighten with His own most admirable light; a Church in which He gives forth mysteries capable of confounding human pride, and yet satisfying an exalted and enlightened humility — truths worthy of the study of the greatest intellects, and yet not cruelly astounding the lowly and the ignorant; a Church condescending with the simple, instructing all, comforting all, cheering and blessing all, whether noble or ignoble, rich or poor, learned or unlearned — making itself, in one word, like St. Paul, " all unto all," that it might gain all to Christ and to His holy religion. And what a religion! How truly divine in its origin and its teachings! How beautifully it accommodates itself to the wants of our poor human nature, whether in its loftiest aspirations or its humblest wishes and desires! What food for the deepest and most exalted contemplation; what comfort for the wearisome ; what consolation for the sorrowful ; what hope for the despondent and strength for the weak !

Our Holy Mother the Church, knowing full well the infirmity of our nature and confidently relying on that infallibility promised to her by her Divine Founder, does not permit her children to be led away by every wind of doctrine or tossed about on every wave of error. Hence it is that she has always deprecated the pernicious principle of *private judgment* in regard to Scriptural interpretation, which principle has been the cause of so much evil, the originator and propagator of every error and heresy that ever disturbed the Christian community.

How fallacious is such a method; how condemnable when examined by the criterion of all ages previous to Luther's unhappy advent; how evidently opposed to Christ's unchangeable truth, contradictory to Scripture, and terribly pernicious in its consequences! Such a principle is at war with the experience of ages and with common sense itself.

That each individual is to form his faith

from a book—divine though it be, yet still a book—intensely deep in its mysteries, difficult of comprehension, having various peculiarities of style, describing times and fashions long since forgotten, using expressions and figures long since obsolete and buried in oblivion—that such a work should be placed in the hands of all indiscriminately for perusal, and the passing of their individual judgment thereon, is the most absurd and preposterous doctrine ever proposed to mankind.

We have only to study the history of the past three centuries in order to become convinced of the vagaries, aberrations, and, I am sorry to say, *abominations* which have been the natural consequence of this doctrine of private judgment.

There is scarcely an error that has ever been conceived in the mind of man, a heresy that has ever been advocated, a doctrine howsoever contradictory or ridiculous, malicious or disgusting, that has not been defended by its promulgators by some texts from Scripture.

As the late Dr. Jebb, the Protestant Bishop of Limerick, declared in one of his sermons: "We find melancholy proof that Bibles, indiscriminately scattered through the land, may be rendered instrumental to the most wicked and infernal purposes. The volume of Scripture is now in every hand, and men without faith, without charity, without God in the world are laboring to convert that volume into the text-book of atheism and anarchy."*

From the time that the Anabaptists deluged Germany with blood, that Hermann announced himself as the Messias and

* Sermon xi.

Joanna Southcote issued her one hundred and forty-four thousand passports to heaven, unto our own days, when the notorious Joe Smith gave unto his so-called "saints" the permission of multiplying the number of their wives, there is no end to the countless offspring of this most prolific principle.

Theory after theory has been launched forth, doctrine after doctrine, sect follows sect, all opposing one another, and yet all resting, or pretending to rest, upon that one corner-stone—the Bible. So that, were we to give any credence to their principle, we would feel ourselves obliged to believe that the Almighty, in giving us the inspired writings, merely gave a *riddle*, and an insolvable one, to the entire human race— which, of course, it would be blasphemy to admit.

According to the aforesaid principle, and

by some strange contradiction impossible to explain, it is perfectly lawful to draw your own creed from the Bible—to believe, with some, that Christ is God, or with others that He was merely a successful moralist and regenerator, that there are three divine persons in the Blessed Trinity, or with others, again, that there is only one; and so on *ad infinitum* in the way of contradictions. As Luther himself said with regard to his own time, and surely it is far more applicable to our age: "*There are as many creeds as there are heads.*" It is perfectly lawful to draw any conclusion, howsoever repugnant, from the Scriptures, provided—and lo! here is the only exception—*provided* you do not find therein that Christ established but *one true Church*, and that that Church is the *Roman Catholic!* Draw any other conclusion but that from the principle of private judgment, and you will certainly be in the way of attaining, as they say, a "blissful immortality!"

So we cannot but perceive the fallacy of such a principle, no matter from what point of view we consider it, and the terrible havoc it has caused for the past three hundred years in the Christian camp. How grateful and happy Catholics ought to be, guided, as they are, by more fixed principles and more stable authority, who cling to the immovable rock of Christ's Holy Church, and rest calm and content amid all the storms of passion, prejudice, and ignorance that beset it on every side! We trust to an authority established and preserved by our Redeemer Himself. It is from it we receive the Divine Book, and it is to that same unfailing authority we look for its rightful interpretation. "Without such a fixed and visible authority," says the amiable and learned Fénelon, " the Christian Church would be like to a republic to which wise laws were given, but without magistrates to look to their execution."

By no other creed is the Bible so much respected and revered as by the Holy Church to which it is our greatest happiness and privilege to belong. From its sacred pages our innumerable martyrs and saints derived strength and consolation, and the Fathers and Doctors of the Church an immense fund of learning and instruction. They considered it the greatest treasure, and mourned over its abuse by those disobedient children who separated themselves from the communion of the faithful. Every Sunday and holiday they read it for the people, and adorned it by their piety and eloquence. It was their study by day; it was their study by night. Many amongst them spent their life, from childhood even unto a venerable age, in drawing forth from its inspired pages lessons of piety and wisdom, not only for themselves, but for countless others committed to their care.

What example more beautiful or more forcible can be found than in the life of the Venerable Bede—the instructor of Alcuin, who, in his turn, became the preceptor of the Emperor Charlemagne—one of the best and most learned of men, who, from lisping infancy even unto old age, devoted himself most ardently to the study of Holy Writ, and expired whilst in the very act of transcribing the last line of the Gospel of St. John?

Long before Luther and his followers

saw the light of day the Church enjoined it as a strict rule on all her clergy and religious orders to recite a considerable part of the Bible every day—different selections being allotted to various seasons and festivals.   Hence in the present age, as in many others preceding, all ecclesiastics in sacred orders are bound, under pain of mortal sin, to recite what is called the Breviary, or Divine Office, every day in the year, unless prevented by sickness or the urgent spiritual necessities of the faithful.

In the olden times the bishops reverently kept the Sacred Scriptures in a safe place at the left side of the main altar, and the Blessed Sacrament on the right side. St. Charles Borromeo and many other saints always read the Bible on their knees.

In all our ecclesiastical educational institutions it is a most special and important part of the studies; and, to give an example of the respect and esteem in which the Bible is held, I shall merely mention that in the seminary of Montreal, in which the writer had the honor of being a student, we were obliged to read a portion of the New Testament every day, on bended knees and with head uncovered, for a considerable length of time. There I have often seen the venerable bishop in his purple robes, the aged superior worn out in the service of God, and the young and delicate student kneel down on the bare floor, modestly take their Testament, and, kissing its sacred · pages with the greatest reverence, proceed, in the strictest silence, to read the holy lessons which it contained. In fact, the faithful ecclesiastic always considers it as his true *vade-mecum.*

The Church, like a prudent and loving mother, wished her children to be preserved from faithless copies of the Bible, and to be put in possession of such only as were duly approved by her and accompanied by appropriate notes and reflections. When she did use restrictive measures it was only when she was compelled to do so by the pressing exigencies of the times, and when the danger had passed she gladly and cheerfully laid aside her apparent severity.

The Jews were always opposed to the indiscriminate reading of the Bible, for it was not permitted for those under thirty years of age to read certain portions of the Old Testament—*v.g.*, the beginning of Genesis, the Canticle of Canticles, and some other special portions of Scripture.

Nor can it be said that the Church was

opposed to the diffusion of the Bible, for it is a well-known fact that in Germany alone, before Luther inaugurated his secession, twenty editions of the Sacred Scriptures had been published. Shortly after the discovery of the art of printing there was published a version which bears no date (as was the case with all the first printed books). Another version appeared in 1467. An edition was printed by Fust in 1472, and a *fifth* edition in 1473, just *ten years before Luther was born.* There were four editions of the Catholic version published in Nuremberg before Luther's version, which was not completed until 1540, made its appearance. According to the late Cardinal Wiseman, a version appeared in Spain A.D. 1478, and in Italy, "the country most peculiarly under the sway of papal dominion, the Scriptures were translated into Italian by Malermi, at Venice, in 1471, and this version was republished seventeen times before the conclusion of that century, and twenty-three years before that of Luther appeared." *

As to translations of the Bible, we have the testimony of the Protestant historian Hallam that long before the art of printing was discovered, "in the eighth and ninth centuries, when the Vulgate had ceased to be generally intelligible, translations were freely made into the vernacular." † Sir Thomas More declared that "the hole Byble was, long before his [Wickliffe's] dayes, by vertuous and wel-lerned men, translated into the English

---

* *Lectures on Catholic Doctrine*, vol. i. page 56, O'Shea's edition.

† *Middle Ages*, vol. iii. p. 424.

tong, and by good and godly people, with devotion and soberness, wel and reverently red." *

So we may easily perceive how utterly baseless as well as malicious are all the slanders uttered against the Catholic Church with regard to her treatment of the sacred volume, so dearly prized by all her children. The Catholic Church is desirous that the Bible should be in the possession of every family and should serve for their instruction and edification, although she knows full well that it is not absolutely necessary for the majority of the people, who can more easily learn the chief truths of religion and the principles of moral conduct from the oral instructions of their pastors. As the great Fénelon so wisely declared, "Christians ought

* *A Dialogue Concernynge Heresyes*, book iii. c. 14.

to be first taught the spirit of the Scriptures before they be permitted to read the letter of the Scriptures. These should only be placed in the hands of simple, docile, and humble souls, who are willing to feast upon them in silence, and not to argue, cavil, and dispute about them; who receive them from the Holy Catholic Church, and only wish to find the true and genuine sense as expounded by this infallible Church, which Jesus Christ commanded us to hear."

Even in this age of steam printing-presses how many millions are yet unable to read; and of those who are able, how few comparatively are capable of understanding many parts of the sacred yet really mysterious book! What deep knowledge is required of ancient languages, the peculiar customs and still more peculiar phraseology of olden times! How many years should be given to study!—and for this would be needed not only ample leisure, but also ample means and no small ability. Then consider how few of the learned, when left to their own lights, agree as to the meaning of the most important texts. In the Epistle of St. Paul to the Galatians there is one very short text, " Now a mediator is not of one; but God is one," * and yet, short as it is, actual count has been made of two hundred and fifty different interpretations with regard to its meaning.

Hence the necessity for the existence of a capable judge; and in matters of such eternal importance there is need of an infallible judge, who will not leave us in darkness nor lead us into error. In

* Gal. iii. 20.

every society, every state, every kingdom or republic there must be a body of laws; if a body of laws, then a court; if a court, then a judge ; and, to settle all difficulties, a court and judge of last resort. Suppose each citizen were permitted to interpret the laws according to his own good pleasure or his own particular judgment, what would be the result ? Anarchy, without shadow of doubt. Allow the same principle in religion, and what would be the consequence ? Rebellion, secession, anarchy, infidelity.

The Bible is the inspired word of God; it is infallible in itself, but it needs an infallible interpreter, and that infallible interpreter can be no other than the one to whom Christ Himself promised that his faith should never fail — St. Peter, the chief of the apostolic band, the centre of unity, the guide, the supporter, the confirmer of his brethren : " I have prayed for thee that thy faith fail not; and thou, being once converted, confirm thy brethren."* " Thou art Peter; and upon this rock I will build my Church, and the gates of hell shall not prevail against it. And I will give to thee the keys of the kingdom of heaven. And whatsoever thou shalt bind upon earth, it shall be bound also in heaven ; and whatsoever thou shalt loose upon earth, it shall be loosed also in heaven." †

Thus we see that the principle of private judgment cannot stand either in Church or state, for it is in reality the principle of insubordination. " He that hath himself for a master," says St. Bernard, " hath a fool for his scholar "; or,

----

* St. Luke xxii. 32.   † St. Matt. xvi. 18, 19.

as a proverb in our day expresses it, " He who is his own lawyer has a fool for his client."

St. Peter, the head of the Apostolic College, declared : " We have not, by following artificial fables, made known to you the power and presence of our Lord Jesus Christ ; but we were eye-witnesses of His greatness.   For He received from God the Father honor and glory ; this voice coming down to Him from the excellent glory : This is my beloved Son, in whom I am well pleased : hear ye Him. And this voice we heard brought from heaven, when we were with Him on the holy mount.   And we have the word of prophecy more firm : to which you do well to attend, as to a light shining in a dark place until the day dawn and the morning star rise in your hearts. *Understanding this first, that no prophecy of the Scrip-ture is made by private interpretation."* It was by forgetting this last injunction of St. Peter that so much disunion was begotten by the unhappy secession of the sixteenth century, and has been ever since wofully on the increase. Cut loose from the Catholic Church and its divine autho-rity, Protestantism has gone on dividing and subdividing, until the number is be-yond count of warring sects that have been sprung upon the religious world to add to its confusion and distraction.

There is a terrible logic in all this ; for if, as they say, Luther and Calvin and the uxorious Harry the Eighth had a right to leave the old Church and to found a new one more in accordance with their tastes and fancies, so each one of their follow-

* 2 St. Peter i. 10–21.

ers has the same right, according to that principle which is the corner-stone of Protestantism—the right of *private judgment.*

They who are outside the one true fold differ not merely in discipline, church government, or in what they call "accidentals," but even as to the fundamental doctrines of Christianity. Hence it is that the so-called popular preachers of the day seldom or never touch upon dogmatic subjects. They do not preach "Christ crucified," but preach themselves, their whims, their fancies, or whatever may be the sensation of the hour—the latest murder, election, discovery, or invention. Even the very mention of the word "dogma" excites such horror that if it were used by a minister of a fashionable congregation it is not unlikely that a committee would be appointed to wait upon him and to warn him that such a term is entirely unsuited to this enlightened nineteenth century, and should only be heard in a Catholic church —"the Church of the dark ages."

"He that believeth not shall be condemned" ("damned," Protestant version), but these sensational preachers say the very opposite: "No matter what you believe or disbelieve, we hail you as brethren." "He that will not hear the Church," says our Lord and Saviour Jesus Christ, "let him be to thee as a heathen and a publican." They say: "Let every man form his own creed and be a church unto himself, and there is no doubt but he will *hear it*," as it will be none other than the personification of his own whims, fancies, theories, or speculations. "Though we, or an angel from heaven, preach a Gospel to you beside that which we have preached to you, let him be anathema," says St. Paul, the great Apostle of the Gentiles.*

They say: "If St. Paul lived in this age he would not be so dogmatic, so intolerant, as such language is now uttered only by the Catholic Church—always, you know, so very dogmatical."

There are not a few preachers in our time—and their number is unfortunately increasing—who no longer believe in the divinity of Christ or in the divine inspiration of the Bible, and yet they hold their ministerial position despite the creeds of their respective denominations. The Rev. Dr. Heber Newton, for instance, a presbyter of the Protestant Episcopal Church, rector of "All Souls'" Church, New York (poor, famished *souls* that ask for the "bread" of true doctrine and are handed

*Galatians i. 8.

" a stone "), calls the belief in the divine inspiration of the Bible " bibliolatry." " It has bred," he says, " a superstitious use of the Bible which has always made mischief, though a mischief never realized so sensibly as now. It has taught men to turn to these holy books and accept unquestioningly all therein recorded as authoritative on our thought and life. It has barred all research which even seemed to contradict its history or science, and has held Europe in mental swaddling-bands, preventing normal growth." · In another place † the same lecturer thus speaks of the Old Testament: " The Old Testament historians contradict each other in facts and figures, tell the same story in different ways, locate the same incident at different periods, ascribe

* *The Right and Wrong Uses of the Bible*, p. 41.
† Page 22.

the same deeds to different men, quote statistics which are plainly exaggerated, mistake poetic legend for sober prose, report the marvellous tales of tradition as literal history, and give us statements which cannot be read as scientific facts without denying our latest and most authoritative knowledge."

We doubt if Robert Ingersoll could say more against the Bible in a paragraph of the same length. Such "ministers of the Gospel" should either resign their positions or, with the consent of their congregations, put the Bible on the shelf and take their Sunday text from Shakspere, or rather from Emerson, the apostle of culture.

The Catholic Church was the preserver and defender of the Bible from the first days of Christianity, as Dr. Newton confesses: " When the writings of Greece and

Rome had been buried in the ruins of the Roman Empire, the literature of Israel was preserved by the pious care of the Christian Church. The light of Athens went out, and the light of Jerusalem alone illumined the dark ages. The only books known to the mass of men through long centuries were these writings of the Hebrews and the early Christians. Thought was kept alive by them, imagination was fed by them, conscience was educated and vitalized through them. For a thousand years there was practically but one book in Europe—the Bible."* In reading other Protestant writers a person would be led to imagine that the Bible was a *hidden book* during all those ages, and that so it remained until Luther discovered it chained to the base of a secret monastic altar.

* *The Right and Wrong Uses of the Bible*, pp. 57, 58.

The Catholic Church, then, was its only guardian in the past, preserving it from the desecrating hands of barbarism, ignorance, and heresy; and the time is fast approaching when she will be its only defender and the only upholder of its divine inspiration in the future.

This nineteenth century is constantly boasting that it is fast burying all the dogmas of the past. The only class of truths it relishes are those that have reference to the mere material world, whatever falls under the observation of the senses, adds to its profits, diminishes its losses, or contributes to its pleasures. All this is in direct opposition to the great maxim of Jesus Christ: "What doth it profit a man if he gain the whole world and lose his own soul?" They who wish to hear the voice of God and secure their eternal happiness must heed the living voice of the Church which He came upon earth to establish, and which He destined to continue His divine work for the salvation of the human race. " We are of God. He that knoweth God hear-eth us; he that is not of God heareth us not. By this we know the Spirit of truth and the spirit of error." *

* 1 St. John iv. 6.

"A CITY that is set on a mountain cannot be hid," * neither can the true Church of God, which is none other than "the holy city the new Jerusalem coming down from God out of heaven, prepared as a bride adorned for her husband." † It is placed thus conspicuously, "the mountain of the house of the Lord," on the "very top of mountains," and "exalted above the hills" of ignorance, prejudice, and passion, so that it cannot fail to be seen by all men who will raise their eyes but for a mo-

* St. Matt. v. 14. † Apoc. xxi. 2.

ment of sober thought from the thinss of earth on which they are constantly bent, and take a steadfast look upon that most magnificent work of the Almighty's creation, "the House of the living God, the pillar and ground of truth."*

From the majestic height whereon it was placed by its All-wise Founder its light radiates over the entire world, even through the darkness of ages, the heavy mists of error, and the poisonous air of heresy. God hath so clothed His Church with beauty and power, and invested it with such striking and resplendent marks of His divine favor and protection, that it cannot fail to impress every sincere seeker after truth with the conviction that it alone possesses those qualities or characteristics which clearly point out the

* 1 Tim. iii. 15.

one true fold of Jesus Christ, the Body of which He is the Head, the Kingdom of which He is the King, the glorious Church, "without spot or wrinkle," of which He is the High-Priest for ever.

The most important of these marks or notes is that perfect *Unity* for which Christ prayed so earnestly that it might be the distinctive characteristic of that Church which He came upon earth to establish and for which He shed His blood. This was to be the sign, during all time, by which His true fold should be known. In that most beautiful, tender, and loving prayer which Jesus offered up to His Heavenly Father, on the eve of His Passion, in behalf of His cherished disciples, He most specially besought for them this great gift of unity: "I do not ask that Thou take them away out of the world, but that Thou preserve them from evil. They are not of the world, as I am not of the world. Sanctify them in truth. Thy word is truth. As Thou hast sent Me into the world, I also have sent them into the world. And for them I do sanctify Myself, that they also may be sanctified in truth. And not for them only do I pray, but for those also who through their word shall believe in Me. *That they all may be one, as Thou, Father, in Me, and I in Thee; that they also may be one in us; that the world may believe that Thou hast sent Me."* *

That Christ's prayers are always heard no Christian can doubt. " Jesus, lifting up His eyes, said : Father, I give Thee thanks that Thou hast heard Me. And

* St. John xvii. 15–22.

I knew that Thou hearest Me always."* That "they may be made perfect in one"† was and is the most earnest wish of our Blessed Lord, and hence unity, perfect unity of faith and doctrine, worship and government, is the essential characteristic of His Holy Church.

The Almighty wished His Church to be like unto Himself—*one.* Being Infinite Truth and Infinite Wisdom personified, His Church should be an image of Himself, and hence should display these wondrous attributes. As God He must necessarily hate error, heresy,. and falsehood of every description. More particularly is this true if these errors or falsehoods regard His own Divine Person, His adorable perfections, His institutions or dispensations. Being the essence of

* St. John xi. 41, 42.　　　† Id. xvii. 23.

truth itself, it is absolutely repugnant to His very nature that He should be indifferent as to doctrines concerning His attributes, His providence, or with regard to the great truths He has vouchsafed to reveal to the human race.

As there is but one God, there can be but one system of divine truth, and consequently but one true religion. God cannot approve of two different religions, much less of a hundred warring creeds, each one contradicting the other on doctrines of the most vital importance; for by so doing He would contradict Himself—a proposition which it would be blasphemous to admit. "Lift up the standard to the people," said the Prophet Isaias;* and the great Apostle St. Paul did indeed lift it up, and wrote upon it characters

* Is. lxii. 10.

that can never fade: "One Lord, one faith, one baptism"—the motto of the Catholic Church, the corner-stone of her doctrinal edifice. This is the great principle on which she was established, the principle on which she works and to which she always clings, unchanging and unchanged.

There is perfect unity in the Godhead —the adorable unity of the Trinity, and a perfect unity in the heavenly hierarchy of the angelic choirs, entire subordination of one order to another, in the rank assigned by the Almighty to His blessed spirits. The most perfect image of this heavenly unity is to be found in the Catholic Church, where it begets beauty, majesty, and strength. This is the only Church which rejoices in the possession of an interior as well as exterior unity. Its interior unity is preserved by the unfailing presence and protection of its Divine Founder: " Behold, I am with you all days, even unto the consummation of the world"; and by the indwelling light and guidance of the Holy Spirit, who is "to abide with it for ever."

The exterior unity of the Church is maintained throughout all ages by the profession by all its members of the same unchangeable faith, by union in worship through the great sacrifice of the Mass—the unbloody renewal of that of Calvary—by the reception of the same grace-giving sacraments, and by unity of government under one divinely-appointed head, the Vicar of Jesus Christ, the successor of St. Peter, the Rock upon which Christ built His Church.

Our Blessed Redeemer always speaks of His Church as but *one:* " On this rock

I will build My Church." Let it be well borne in mind He does not say *churches.* Whenever He refers to it it is always the *one Church,* the *one fold,* under *one shepherd,* the *one kingdom.* " He that will not hear *the Church,* let him be to thee as the heathen and the publican." * " Other sheep I have, that are not of this fold; them also I must bring, and they shall hear my voice, and there shall be *one fold* and *one* shepherd." † The apostles always understood it in the same sense, and expressed themselves strongly and clearly on this point : " We, being many, are *one body* in Christ." ‡ " One Lord, one faith, one baptism." § In one Spirit are we all baptized into *one body,* whether Jews or Gentiles, bond or free." |

* St. Matt. xviii. 17.　† St. John x. 16.　‡ Rom. xii. 5.
§ Eph. iv. 5.　　　| 1 Cor. xii. 13.

"Careful to keep the unity of the spirit in the bond of peace. *One body* and *one Spirit*, as you are called in *one hope* of your calling." * " Christ is the Head of the Church ; He is the saviour of His body." † According to this same chapter of St. Paul's Epistle to the Ephesians, the Church is the spouse of Christ, always subject and ever faithful to Him, loved and cherished by Him in return, and bound to Him by a union that can never be dissolved—" a glorious Church without spot or wrinkle." This spouse was prefigured in the Canticle of Canticles : " One is my dove, my perfect one is but one. . . . Who is she that cometh forth as the morning rising, fair as the moon, bright as the sun, terrible as an army set in array ?" ‡ The " morning rising " of the Church took

* Eph. iv. 3, 4.   † Eph. v. 23.   ‡ Cant. vi. 8, 9.

place in the time of the patriarchs; "fair as the moon" did it become under the rule of Moses and the prophets; "bright as the sun" from the days of Jesus Christ, the Sun of Justice, and "terrible as an army set in array" to all its enemies—infidels, heretics, schismatics.

Unity of doctrine has always been the most resplendent mark of Christ's true Church. In every place and in every age she has always taught the same divine truths that were handed down by Christ and His Apostles, and contained in the Sacred Scriptures or the apostolic traditions. For we know full well that many things which Christ did and said were not committed to writing by His disciples, but delivered by word of mouth to the various assemblies which they addressed, and more particularly and more fully to those whom they ordained to the ministry. " There are also many other things which Jesus did, which if they were written every one," says the Beloved Disciple, St. John, at the close of his Gospel, " the world itself, I think, would not be able to contain the books that should be written."

How many instructions of the greatest importance must not the apostles have received from their Divine Master during the forty days that He spent upon earth from the time of His Resurrection until His Ascension, preparing them for their great mission of "teaching all nations"! And most assuredly all these instructions were not committed to writing. Even in the Old Law some of the most important doctrines, such as the Trinity, immortality of the soul, and other truths, are not fully expressed in the writings of the Old Testament, but were handed down by word of mouth by the Jewish priests and doctors of the law to those persons who were to succeed them in office. The late Cardinal Wiseman said that "those who will take the requisite pains to trace the doctrines of the Jews in this regard will find that from the very beginning, from the delivery of the law to Moses, there was a great mass of precepts not written, but committed to the keeping of the priesthood, and by them gradually communicated or diffused among the people, but yet hardly alluded to in the writings of the Sacred Book." He then refers to the works of the learned Molitor, of Frankfort, on *The Philosophy of History or Tradition*—a distinguished author, who, "educated in the Jewish religion, had made himself perfect master of all the writings of the Jews, and who, it is evident from the whole line of argument that pervades his work, was brought to the Catholic religion, and is now one of its defenders, simply from finding that among the Jews there was a series of traditions which received its development only in Catholic Christianity, and a sacred system of mystical theology which has been manifestly preserved and continued." * "In the first page of one of their most esteemed and most ancient treatises (*Pirke Aboth*)," says the same eminent writer, "it is expressly stated that Moses received on Sinai, besides the written, an oral and traditional revelation, which he delivered to the priests."

St. Paul strongly exhorts the Thessalo-

---

* Lecture III., on "Principal Doctrines of the Catholic Church."

nians : " Hold the traditions which you have learned, whether by word or our epistle." * " Hold the form of sound words which thou hast heard from me in faith," the same apostle says to St. Timothy. † " And the things which thou hast learned from me before many witnesses, the same commend to faithful men, who shall be fit to teach others also." ‡

There has been but one set of doctrines handed down to us by Christ, contained in the Word of God, either written in the Scriptures or unwritten and preserved in sacred tradition. There has been no change from age to age, for the very same doctrines that are now taught by the Catholic Church in this nineteenth century are the same as were taught in the sixteenth, the tenth, the fifth, or the

* 2 Epist. ii. 14.　　† 2 Epist. i. 13.　　‡ Ib. ii. 2.

first. We hold absolutely to the same creeds—the Apostles' Creed, the Nicene, the Athanasian, that of Pope Pius IV., and that of the Vatican. There is no essential change of doctrine in all these ages, but there is a natural development, a fuller setting forth and clearer enunciation of truths already believed, which places them beyond the possibility of dispute. Doctrines may be, and have been, more clearly defined, but this by no means argues a change in the doctrines themselves. The little child of a few months who in course of time develops into the full-grown man is one and the same personality. As St. Vincent of Lerins says: "Shall there be no progress in the Church of Christ? There shall be progress, and even great progress; for who would be so envious of the good of men, or so cursed of God, as to prevent it? But it will be *progress*, and not *change*. With the growth of the ages and centuries there must necessarily be a growth of intelligence, wisdom, and knowledge for each man as well as for all the Church. But the religion of souls must imitate the progress of the human form, which, in developing and growing with years, never ceases to be the same in the maturity of age as in the flower of youth." *

The divinity of Christ was proclaimed a dogma of the Church in the Council of Nice, A.D. 325; and most assuredly this was not a new doctrine, for it was the very foundation of Christianity, and yet it was thus clearly defined in order to preserve the faithful from the snares of the Arian heretics, and to unmask these

* *Commonitorium Peregrini.*

wolves in sheep's clothing, who were insidiously endeavoring to undermine the true Christian faith. Neither the whole Church in council assembled, nor even its Supreme Head, can proclaim a new doctrine or pretend to a new revelation in this respect, but merely decide what is contained in the original deposit of faith handed down by Christ and His apostles. The great principle of the Catholic Church is, "*Nihil quod non traditum est*"—"Nothing but what has been handed down" by Christ and His disciples can be held as of faith in the Catholic Church.

The belief in the Immaculate Conception of the Blessed Virgin Mary is consequently as old as Christianity itself, although it was not solemnly declared a dogma, which we are bound to believe under pain of excommunication, until the

year 1854. Before proclaiming this truth
as a dogma Pope Pius IX. consulted the
bishops of the entire Catholic world as to
what was always the firm belief of the
faithful on this point in their respective
dioceses; and, having received satisfactory
answers, he, the Supreme Pontiff, to the
joy of all the faithful, solemnly defined
that Mary was conceived without the stain
of original sin, through the preventing
grace and merits of Jesus Christ. When
the Almighty pronounced judgment on
Satan, who had assumed the form of a
serpent, He said: " I will put enmities between thee and the woman, and thy seed
and her seed; she shall crush thy head,
and thou shalt lie in wait for her heel." *
Mary, through the merits of her Divine
Son, crushed Satan by her sinless concep-

* Genesis iii. 15.

tion. This dogma has the closest connection with that of the divinity of Christ. For surely it would reflect no honor on Him were His Mother subject, even for a moment, to the power and influence of Satan, His avowed enemy; and subject undoubtedly she would have been had she been born in the state of original sin. That Christ was both willing and able to make His Mother an exception with regard to this hereditary taint the Catholic Church has never for an instant doubted; and it is, indeed, hard to believe that any one who sincerely loves and adores Jesus Christ can have any difficulty in taking such a doctrine to his mind and heart. There is a very large number of non-Catholics in our times that hold that no child of Adam is born in original sin, hence they certainly cannot object to

Catholic teaching on this point. Nor is it a new doctrine even on this great continent, for some two hundred years ago chapels in honor of the Immaculate Conception were erected in different parts of America. The great apostolic missionary as well as discoverer, Father James Marquette, the Jesuit, in the year 1673 discovered the Mississippi and called it the " River of the Immaculate Conception." " I put our voyage," he himself wrote, " under the protection of the Blessed Virgin Immaculate, promising her that if she did us the grace to discover the great river I would give it the name of Conception." *

As with the Immaculate Conception, so also with regard to the dogma of Papal

* Dr. Gilmary Shea's *Discovery and Exploration of the Mississippi.*

Infallibility—the doctrine comes down to us from Christ Himself, on whose very words it is founded: " Simon, Simon, behold Satan hath desired to have you that he may sift you as wheat. But I have prayed for thee that thy faith fail not ; and thou being once converted, confirm thy brethren." * These solemn words have been understood in the same sense in every age, as may clearly be seen from the writings and testimonies of the Fathers and Doctors of the Catholic Church.

The teachings, then, of the Church have never undergone any essential change in any age or clime, and the very same doctrines are proposed to the learned as well as to the unlearned, to kings as well as to beggars, to philosophers and scientists as well as to the illiterate and simple-minded,

* St. Luke xxii. 31, 32,

and are to be found in the smallest cate-
chism as well as in the voluminous works
of our deepest theologians.

The great Fathers of the Church in
every age have always insisted on unity
of doctrine as an essential mark or characteristic of the true religion of Jesus
Christ. A few quotations will suffice.
St. Augustine says: " All the assemblies,
or rather divisions, that call themselves
churches of Christ, but which, in fact,
have separated themselves from the congregation of unity, do not belong to the
true Church. · They might, indeed, belong
to her if the Holy Ghost could be divided
against Himself ; but as this is impossible,
they do not belong to her."*

Origen—that marvel of learning—thus
speaks: " As there are many who fancy

* *De Verbo Domini*, serm. ii.

that they think the things of Christ, and some of them think differently from those that went before, let there be preserved the ecclesiastical teaching which, transmitted by the order of succession from the apostles, remains even to the present day in the churches ; 'that alone is to be believed as truth which in nothing differs from the ecclesiastical and apostolical tradition." *

" They again must be reproved, whoever they are," says St. Ephraem, a Syrian confessor of the fourth century, " who go astray out of the highway, and wander along devious and treacherous paths ; seeing that the way of salvation presents to us marks whereby we may perfectly know that this is the road which the messengers of peace trod ; which the wise, inspired . by the

* * De. Principiis.*

Spirit, hath foreshown, and which the prophets and apostles have left us levelled and made smooth ; whose milestones truth has set up, and whose hostelries Christ has fitted up. Come, brethren, let us enter upon this road, by which the Father sent the Son ; let us keep to the King's highway, that we may all journey together even to the beholding of the King's Son." *

St. Cyprian, the great Bishop of Carthage, who suffered martyrdom A.D. 258, wrote an entire work on the Unity of the Church, from which we take this short extract : " There is but one God, and one Christ, and one faith, and a people joined in one solid body with the cement of concord. This unity cannot suffer a division, nor can this one body bear to be disjoint-

* Serm. xxv. adv. Hæres.

ed. He cannot have God for his Father who has not the Church for his Mother. If any one could escape the deluge out of Noe's ark, he who is out of the Church may also escape. To abandon the Church is a crime which blood cannot wash away. Such a one may be put to death, but he cannot be crowned."

The Protestant Bishop Pearson admits the same, and almost in the same words: "Christ never appointed two ways to heaven; nor did He build a Church to save some, and make another institution for other men's salvation. As none were saved from the deluge but such as were in the ark of Noe, so none shall ever escape the eternal wrath of God which belong not to the Church of God."* This, certainly, was a strong condemnation of

* *Exposition of the Creed*, p. 349.

his own position and of that of the Church by law established.

It is reported that Bishop Jewel, of the same establishment, made the very strange and ridiculous charge against the Catholic Church that it was wanting in unity because some friars *dressed in black, others in brown;* some in *white*, others again in *blue;* some lived on meat, others on fish and vegetables! Surely this does not constitute division on points of doctrine. It is also objected by ignorant persons that the Church is divided into the different camps of Jesuits, Dominicans, Franciscans, Augustinians, and Benedictines; but, as every educated man knows, or ought to know, these orders do not hold different forms of faith, but simply have different rules of community life. Every Catholic, whether a member of an order or not, Jesuit or

Dominican, bishop or priest, pope or layman, must subscribe to the same unchangeable rule of faith; and no matter what his rank, learning, talents, or position, if he deny but one dogma of the Catholic religion he is *ipso facto* cut off from the communion of the faithful. Considering the frailty of human nature and the perversity of the human will, "there must be also heresies," says St. Paul,* "that they also who are reproved may be made manifest among you." Heresies, like scandals, shall arise, but woe to them through whom they come!

T. W. Allies, the distinguished English author, gave the following beautiful testimony to the unity of doctrine of the Catholic Church, some years before he resigned his position in the Established

---

* 1 Cor. xi. 19.

Church and joined our communion: "This body of doctrine is uniform, coherent, systematic, forming a whole which comprehends all the relations of man to God from the formation of the first man to the general judgment of the world. These bishops, and the priests under them, are not in the habit of disputing what this body of doctrine is; for, as to all that concerns the Christian life, it has long ago been clearly defined and established. In the long course of eighteen hundred years disputes about it have indeed arisen; they have then been terminated by common consent; individuals who took a different view about them from the whole body have been obliged to leave it, and the truth has only come out the more sharply defined from these contests. Moreover, as this doctrine claims to be *revealed*, and as all revelation must be partial, as a light shining amid darkness, penetrating it, indeed, on all sides, but leaving indefinite spaces beyond unillumined, there are a multitude of questions more or less touching on this doctrine, yet not comprehended in it or decided by it. Only enough is, by the consent of all members of this hierarchy, decided so as to leave the Christian in no doubt as to any point concerning his salvation or as to any practical means of obtaining it. There is no split in this doctrine, dividing its professors into different camps ; no internal opposition of principles reproduced in external divisions. It is one logical whole. If fresh doubts as to any point not yet decided be raised by the ever-active intellect of man, then the hierarchy, either collectively or by tacit adherence to the voice of its chief, declares and decides the point mooted. This body of doctrine, thus possessed and taught by this hierarchy, is termed *the Faith*, and it is necessary for every simple member of the communion to hold and believe it. It is clear that no such body of doctrine could exist without a power co-existing at all times to declare what does or does not belong to it; for were it simply written in a book, interminable disputes would arise as to the meaning of the book—just as the English law, the work of ages, exists in a great number of volumes, but requires no less for its practical daily working the decision of a supreme judicial authority. The sovereign declares in his courts of justice what is *the law;* the Church declares in her court what is *the Faith.* This, in civil matters, is government; in spiritual it is infallibility; without it, in the state, there would be no one authority, in the Church no one belief; this would be dissolved in anarchy, and that distracted by heresy." *

No other Church possesses this unity of doctrine. All heresies must seek some other abiding-place. Ninety distinct heresies sprang up in the first four hundred years of the Church's history, ninety from then until Luther's advent, two hundred and seventy in the sixteenth century, and how many have since arisen it is almost impossible to enumerate. It is estimated that there are at the present time one hundred and fifty different sects in England; and as to the number of denominations in this country, a new census would be necessary every year to arrive at a close estimate.

* *A Life's Decision*, pp. 255–257.

None of the Protestant sects of the present day hold to the doctrines of the first "Reformers." Even the first Protestants widely disagreed among themselves, even with regard to important points of doctrine. Zwingle separated from Luther and became the leader of the Sacramentarians. Muncer and Storck, carrying out logical deductions from Luther's principles, advocated the abrogation of all law and authority, and were in favor of absolute communism. "At the present day," says Father Nampon, "even in Calvin's own city, his authority is completely annihilated, and the prevailing theology is thoroughly anti-Calvinistic. As a man, Calvin has been exposed to public contempt by Galliffe; as a politician, he has seen his work utterly destroyed by Fazy; as a theologian, he has been convicted of absurdity and immorality by Chenèvriere." Since Nampon wrote the above the ministers of Geneva have thrown off all disguise and are now avowed rationalists. So stands what has been called the "Protestant Rome." How many educated Protestants could now be found who would, without any mental reservation, subscribe to the Articles of Smalcald, the Synod of Dort, the Augsburg Confession, the Westminster Confession, or the Thirty-nine Articles?

The chief doctrine of Luther, and, in fact, the very corner-stone of doctrinal Protestantism at the opening of the so-called "Reformation," was *justification by faith alone;* and yet it was rejected by the Arminians, Socinians, the Wesleyan Methodists, and, so far as I have been able to learn, is nowhere preached in our day. "Hold fast to this doctrine of justification by faith alone," says Luther. " If we lose it we shall no longer be in a condition to resist the devil and the pope, much less to vanquish them." Protestants, as a body, have come over to the Pope's side on this question, and believe in the necessity of faith showing itself in good works, or, in other words, of faith working through charity.

"The Church," says Father Nampon, S.J., " to which at its first rise the Reformation had attributed the right of judging the pope, bishops, and councils, soon finds itself deprived of its priesthood, which is declared to be common to all Christians ; deprived of its power, which it abdicates into the hands of the state ; deprived of its sacraments, which the rationalists take from it one after another, to such a point that at the present day, according to Newman, one-half the people of England are not baptized ; deprived of its worship, which, being at first reduced to an optional attendance at a preaching, is now almost entirely done away with by the progress of individualism ; in fine, it becomes in its own eyes something so uncertain and so vague that Protestantism has never hitherto been able to find a definition of the Church on which it could rest. It must now despair of ever finding one. The grand palladium of the Reformers, the Scripture itself—that Scripture so ill-treated in the translations of Luther and Beza—is from the very first an object of contempt to the Anabaptist enthusiasts and the mystics. Theobald Thamer prefers to it conscience, *which is God Himself.* In Hobarg's eyes it is *an old, dead, and chilly thing,* which can only make

Pharisees. At a later period the Arminians deny the inspiration of the historical books. Then comes the rationalistic exegesis, which leaves nothing in the Bible untouched. Authenticity, integrity, truth, inspiration—all is made matter of question, all is denied." *

Protestant doctrines, according to Schleiermacher, last, on an average, only *fifteen years;* so that, according to this estimate, it would require an abler and more industrious writer than the immortal Bossuet to keep count of the never-ending "variations" from his time to this, the latter part of the nineteenth century. If he had been able to fill two large volumes in relating the *Variations of the Protestant Churches* up to his time, how many volumes would now be required we leave

* *Catholic Doctrine of the Council of Trent*, pp. xix., xx.

to the conjecture of others to determine. "The corner-stone of Protestantism," says a non-Catholic writer in the *Westminster Review* for July, 1872, "is an admirable one for a temple of free thought and nothing else." This is lamentably true, and the worst effect produced by its endless dissensions is that there is a growing disregard for all dogmatic truth. Heresy does not now produce that abhorrence which it should in every Christian heart, that should be desirous of preserving intact the seamless robe of Jesus Christ. Let the distinction be well understood that we should *hate heresy* in every shape and form, but we should not hate *heretics*, whose sad lot we should rather commiserate, and strive, by word, by example, by prayer and the exercise of Christian charity, to lead them to their Father's home through the rich pastures of the one true fold of Jesus Christ.

We by no means rejoice, but rather grieve, over the terrible falling-away from fundamental Christian truths that has taken place in the ranks of those who are at least nominally Protestant. A very large number of them believe no longer in the Trinity, the divinity of Christ, the doctrine of original sin, the existence of hell, or even the inspiration of the Scriptures. In all this they are but carrying out, with remorseless logic, the principles of the self-styled " Reformers." " I consider myself the most rational of Protestants," wrote the infidel Bayle to Polignac, " because, led by Protestant principles, I protest equally against all systems and all sects." " Prove to me," said Jean Jacques Rousseau, " that I am bound to obey authority in religion, and to-morrow I will become a Catholic."

The Germans are considered deep philosophers and good logicians, and hence Protestantism has led them to rationalism pure and simple. Only a very small percentage of the non-Catholic population of the great German nation, more particularly that of Berlin and the other chief cities, attend religious services of any kind whatsoever. As to the condition of Protestantism, we here give the testimony of Schérer, a distinguished Protestant: "This church, deprived alike of its corporate and its dogmatic character, of its form and of its doctrine, deprived of all that constituted it a Christian church and distinguished it as a particular church, has, in truth, ceased to exist in the ranks of religious communities. Its name continues, but it represents only a corpse, a phantom, or, if you will, a memory or a hope. . . . Our faculties of theology teach orthodoxy and rationalism without distinction. A given professor can, without control and without being unfaithful to his engagements, overthrow revealed religion by criticism, and natural religion by speculation. Pastors enjoy the same latitude. They are opposed one to another, and so likewise are the churches, and even consistories. We have no longer any ecclesiastical institutions, properly so called, nor unity nor religious government. . . . For want of a dogmatic authority unbelief has made its way into three-fourths of our pulpits."*

That the Established Church of England is not in much better condition we may easily infer from the description given by

* *De l'État actuel de l'Église réformée en France.*

one who knows it well—Cardinal John Henry Newman : " We see in the English church, I will not merely say no descent from the first ages, and no relationship to the Church in other lands, but we see no body politic of any kind ; we see nothing more or less than an Establishment, a department of government, or a function or operation of the state, without a substance—a mere collection of officials, depending on and living in the supreme civil power. Its unity and personality are gone, and with them its power of exciting feelings of any kind. . . . Bishop is not like bishop more than king is like king or ministry like ministry; its Prayer-Book is an Act of Parliament of two centuries ago, and its cathedrals and its chapter-houses are the spoils of Catholicism. I have said all this, not in declamation, but to bring out clearly why I cannot feel interest of any kind in the national church, nor put any trust in it at all from its past history, as if it were, in however narrow a sense, a guardian of orthodoxy. It is as little bound by what it said or did formerly as this morning's newspaper by its former numbers, except as it is bound by the law; and while it is upheld by the law it will not be weakened by the subtraction of individuals nor fortified by their continuance. Its life is an Act of Parliament. It will not be able to resist the Arian, Sabellian, or Unitarian heresies, because Bull or Waterland resisted them a century or two before; nor, on the other hand, would it be unable to resist them, though its more orthodox theologians were presently. to leave it. It will be able to resist them while the state gives the

word; it would be unable when the state
forbids it. Elizabeth boasted that she
'tuned her pulpits'; Charles forbade dis-
cussions on predestination, George on the
Holy Trinity; Victoria allows differences
on Holy Baptism." *

How earnestly did not the blessed Apostles warn Christians against all heresies
and schisms! "Take heed, brethren,"
says St. Paul to the Hebrews, † "lest
there be in any of you an evil heart
of unbelief, to depart from the living
God." "Mark them," he says to the
Romans, ‡ "who cause dissensions and
offences contrary to the doctrine which
you have learned, and avoid them."
St. Peter, chief of the apostles, also
warns the faithful against teachers of error

* *Anglican Difficulties*, p. 4.   † Heb. iii. 12.
‡ Rom. xvi. 17.

and heresy : "There shall be lying teachers among you, who shall bring in sects of perdition " * (or *damnable heresies*, according to the Protestant version). " These are fountains without water, and clouds tossed with whirlwinds, to whom the mist of darkness is reserved." † St. Paul clearly prophesies the advent of heretics : " Now the Spirit manifestly saith that in the last times some shall depart from the faith, giving heed to spirits of error and doctrines of devils, speaking lies in hypocrisy, and having their conscience seared." ‡

We thus see from different parts of the Sacred Scripture that heresy is a great sin and a great evil, which should be avoided by every man desirous of his salvation. All schisms and dissensions are also strongly condemned by the apostles. The mis-

* 2 Ep. ii. 1.　　　† Id. 17.　　　‡ 1 Tim. iv. 1, 2.

fortune of this age, or rather, to call things by their proper names, the crime of the age, is to think lightly of, or to disregard totally, all supernatural truth, and to reject even the few Christian dogmas that were retained by the "Reformers." And yet but lately the entire Protestant world celebrated with great demonstrations of joy the fourth centenary of Luther's birth. How few of those who rejoiced, or pretended to rejoice, would be able to give a satisfactory reason for so doing! For many can be found who, though nominally Protestant, yet do not hold the doctrines taught by Martin Luther. If he were to return to earth he would find it extremely difficult, if not altogether impossible, to recognize his spiritual offspring. A still larger number are ignorant as to the real character of Luther and his associates, the dubious methods they used to carry their ends, their quarrels and dissensions, the contradictions to be found in their writings, and the sad deterioration in morals acknowledged even by themselves to have been produced by their rejection of the authority of the Catholic Church.

Having carefully and calmly read the writings of many Protestant as well as Catholic authors on this subject, I here set down naught in malice, but endeavor to the best of my ability to serve the interests of truth, which should be dear to every man.

Martin Luther was a man of great natural ability and not devoid of some good qualities. He received an excellent education, possessed energy. of character, was gifted with eloquence and inclined to

piety. But his piety, which began by
being over-scrupulous, ended in wayward-
ness, as piety of that peculiar kind generally does. Sometimes he was careless as
to the fulfilment of his obligations, more
particularly that of the daily recitation of
the Breviary, or Divine Office (chiefly
composed of appropriate selections from
the Sacred Scriptures); and then he would
go to the other extreme and punish himself by excessive austerities and corporal
scourging in order to atone for his delin-
quencies. For this he was often censured
by his superiors; yet he heeded not their
counsel, and was therefore wanting in that
strict obedience demanded by rule of every
monk. With this exception I see no reason to doubt that Dr. Martin Luther was
for a few years an earnest, studious, and
mortified priest and monk, and that he felt

sincerely grieved at the worldly, disedifying conduct of many of the clergy of his time, more particularly of those in exalted rank. There certainly was sufficient ground for complaint and much need of reform not only in the sixteenth century, but also in the preceding ages. Nor was Luther the first to perceive it; for far greater and holier men, like St. Gregory VII., St. Peter Damian, St. Bernard, Cardinal Julian, Cardinal Cusanus, and other eminent churchmen, wrote and worked and prayed for a reformation of morals and the re-establishment of proper discipline amongst the members of the clergy. * The ground had been long preparing for the sowing of the seed of revolt. The people had not been well instructed in

---

* It is well to note, however, that the disorders among the clergy grew out of lay usurpation of pontifical rights.

their faith; kings and princes were rest-
less under the yoke of papal supervision,
and only too anxious for a pretext to rob
the monasteries and to seize on Church
property. Many others were desirous of
being freed from all restraint in the indulgence of their passions, and hence
when the great conflagration burst forth
it was not entirely caused by Luther's action. He struck the spark, it is true, but
then he found the material, the shavings
and kindling, all ready for the fire.

The occasion or first apparent motive
that Luther had for beginning his revolt
was, at bottom, only jealousy, because another religious order — namely, the Dominican — received the appointment to
preach the Papal Indulgence. As many
of our Protestant friends have the strang-
est misconceptions as to this point of Ca-

tholic doctrine, a few words on "indulgences" will not here be out of place.

Protestants, and, generally speaking, all non-Catholics, owing to bitter prejudices in which they have been brought up, and their consequent ignorance of Catholic teaching, are under an impression that *an indulgence means a permission to commit sin.* Such undoubtedly was the belief of the great mass of Protestants in days gone by, and, strange to say, there is still a large number of persons, especially among the uneducated living in retired country districts, who yet hold this ridiculous notion. It is scarcely necessary to say, it is to be hoped, that no Catholic believes such an abominable doctrine. Certainly neither the Catholic Church nor its head upon earth, the Pope, can do what God Himself cannot do—namely, give permis-

sion to any one to commit sin. Let any
one of my Protestant readers stop the first
Catholic child he meets and ask him the
meaning of an indulgence, or examine any
of our catechisms, and he will receive this
answer: "An indulgence is a release from
the temporal punishment due to sin, *after
its guilt has been remitted* in the tribunal
of penance."

This certainly is very plain. Protestants,
if I mistake not, believe that when their
sins are forgiven the punishment due to
those sins is likewise remitted. Not so
Catholics. We believe that a true, heartfelt sorrow as well as a firm purpose of
amendment are absolutely necessary in
order to obtain pardon; and when our
sins are forgiven we believe also that the
eternal punishment due to them is remitted likewise, but ·that some *temporal pun-*

ishment remains to be undergone either in this life or in the next. David certainly knew that his sins were forgiven, since he was assured of the fact by God's prophet ; and yet that same prophet, Nathan, declared to him that he would have to suffer a grievous temporal punishment in consequence : " David said to Nathan : I have sinned against the Lord. And Nathan said to David : The Lord also hath taken away thy sin ; thou shalt not die. Nevertheless, because thou hast given occasion to the enemies of the Lord to blaspheme, for this thing the child that is born to thee shall surely die." *

In the primitive ages of the Church those persons who were guilty of certain grievous and scandalous sins were obliged to undergo public penance for weeks,

*2 Kings xii. 13, 14.

months, and sometimes even years. It now and then happened, through the mediation or intercession of some holy confessors suffering in chains for the faith, that these penitents obtained a release from this canonical penance. This release was of the nature of an *indulgence;* and, therefore, when the Church announces, for instance, an indulgence of forty days or two hundred days for some work of devotion performed with proper dispositions, this means a release from temporal punishment equivalent to the canonical penance formerly inflicted for that definite portion of time. A plenary indulgence, if the dispositions of the penitent be perfect, releases from all the temporal punishment due to the sins already forgiven. That the Church has this power of loosening as well as binding is evident from the words of Christ, her Founder, to St. Peter, and in him to his successors : " I will give to thee the keys of the kingdom of heaven ; and whatsoever thou shalt bind upon earth, it shall be bound also in heaven ; and whatsoever thou shalt loose upon earth, it shall be loosed also in heaven." * The Holy Catholic Church has power, therefore, to impose penalties and to withdraw them when she deems proper.

St. Paul exercised this power when he excommunicated the incestuous Corinthian : " I indeed absent in body, but present in spirit, have already judged, as though I were present, him that hath so done, in the name of our Lord Jesus Christ, you being gathered together and my spirit, with the power of our Lord Jesus, to deliver such a one to Satan for

* St. Matt. xvi. 19.

the destruction of the flesh, that the spirit may be saved in the day of our Lord Jesus Christ." * There is nothing more terrible in this life than this form of excommunication used by St. Paul; and yet out of the goodness of his apostolic heart, on the repentance of this sinner and for the sake of the faithful Corinthians, he granted him an indulgence or a release from this terrible temporal punishment : " For your sakes have I done it in the person of Christ." †

If St. Paul had this power, then, without doubt, St. Peter, the chief of the apostles, possessed it ; and if St. Peter had it, so also his successors in office are endowed with the same power. They do no more and no less than St. Paul did on the occasions referred to in Sacred Writ.

* 1 Cor. v. 3–6.   † 2 Cor. ii. 10.

But some one may ask, Were there not abuses connected with the proclamation of indulgences in the time of Luther? There may have been some exaggeration in the mode of preaching them by some of the friars, but the Church was not to blame, nor the doctrine itself of indulgences. Every good thing is liable to abuse. Liberty, free-will, the Bible are all good things in themselves, yet how fearfully are they not abused! The Catholic Church teaches that no indulgence can be gained by any one in the state of mortal sin or out of the friendship of God. Hence true sorrow for past sins, a firm purpose of change of life, a clear confession and restitution or reparation of injuries done, are all necessary for forgiveness, and before any indulgence can possibly be gained. Even Tetzel, the Dominican preacher of the Papal Indulgence, whom Luther attacked so bitterly, laid down these same conditions in his instruction to parish priests, October 31, 1517: " Whosoever, having confessed and being penitent (*confessus et contritus*), shall bring alms (*eleemosynam*), shall obtain remission of temporal and canonical punishment."

The granting of indulgences, especially in the form of a Jubilee, has always been productive of immense good in the improvement of morals, the awakening of piety, the increase of devotion, and the multiplication of works of charity. Pope Clement VI., in his bull announcing the Jubilee of 1350, declared: " We grant these indulgences to the end that the piety of the Roman people and of all the faithful may be increased, that their faith

may shine with greater lustre, their hope
become more firm, their charity more active and fervent."

Father Nampon, in his excellent work
on the *Catholic Doctrine of the Council
of Trent*, says : " The *fruit* of an indulgence is to remove from us the pains of
this life, or at least to take from them
the aggravating character of *punishments*,
and to accelerate our entrance into glory
by assisting us to discharge all our debts.
Assuredly nothing can be more advantageous to us.   While by this motive the
faithful are encouraged to profit by indulgences, the just detained in purgatory receive the benefit of those which we gain
for them.   These suffering souls are no
longer under the jurisdiction of the
Church militant ; she cannot, therefore, deliver them directly from their debt, but

she may, by offering to God the equivalent of what they owe, ask and more
readily obtain their deliverance. This is
what is called applying an indulgence to
the dead by way of suffrage ; and it is
one of the sweetest and most consoling
consequences of the communion of saints.
' The souls of the faithful departed are
not separated from the Church,' says St.
Augustine ;* ' otherwise there would not
be a commemoration made of them at
the altar of God in the communication of
the Body of Christ.' If, by his prayers,
his alms, his satisfactory works, offered for
the benefit of the dead, a simple believer
can obtain from God the alleviation of
their sufferings, far stronger reason have
we to believe that this power of intercession belongs to the visible head of the

* *De Civit. Dei*, l. xx. c. 9.

Church, who is established by Jesus Christ as the minister of reconciliation, the dispenser of the divine mysteries, the depository of the keys of the kingdom of heaven." *

"What a magnificent picture," says De Maistre, "is that of this immense commonwealth of spirits with its three orders ever in relation with one another! The world which is *engaged in the combat* holds out one hand to the world of *sufferers*, and seizes with the other that of the world of *those in triumph*. Thanksgiving, prayer, satisfactions, aid, inspirations, faith, hope, love circulate from one to the other as beneficent streams. Nothing is isolated, and the souls, like the plates of a galvanic battery, enjoy both their own strength and that of all the others."

* Page 632.

It may be asked, Was there not question of money in connection with indulgences? Yes, there was, but the money was given, or should only have been given or asked, in the form of alms for a worthy object. It was by means of these alms that asylums, hospitals, and churches were built, and that armies were assisted in their defence of Christendom against the Turks. In Luther's time these offerings were given for the completion of St. Peter's Church at Rome, "the cathedral of all Christendom," as Wendell Phillips calls it. Even in our day, when a Jubilee is proclaimed there are boxes placed in every church for the reception of the offerings of the faithful, and these alms are distributed to the poor, devoted to the support of orphans or to the propagation of the faith in pagan countries.

To set a price on anything sacred, whether sacraments or indulgences, would be the sacrilegious crime of simony, so abhorred by the Church. So, then, on the ground of indulgences, there was no reason for seceding from the Catholic Church, since it condemned the abuses to which Luther referred. He himself in the beginning did not attack the doctrine of indulgences, for when he nailed his ninety-five propositions to the door of the church of Wittenberg, October 31, 1517, he declared in his thirty-first proposition: " Whosoever speaks against the truths of papal indulgences, let him be anathema." * In defending his theses he professed entire obedience to the pope, Leo X., saying in his letter : " Most Holy Father, I cast myself at thy feet, with all that I have and

* Vide Alzog's *History*, vol. iii. p. 13.

am. Give life or take it ; call, recall, approve, reprove ; your voice is that of Christ, who presides and speaks in you." As events soon showed, he was not sincere in these sentiments; for as soon as the pope, who treated Luther with great forbearance, condemned his false propositions, he received in return only vile abuse.

Many writers hold that the cause of the " Reformation " may be traced to the great corruption existing in the Church at that time ; but the Protestant historian Guizot, in his *History of European Civilization*, declares " it is not true that in the sixteenth century abuses, properly so called, were more numerous, more crying, than they had been at other times."

Even if such corruption, as alleged, really did exist, this was no reason for abandon-

ing the Church in order to reform it. It
would be just as sensible for a person
who wished to clean or renovate the *interior* of his house to put himself on the
outside and then fling dirt at it. Great
saints clamored for reform, and in so
doing they knew full well that the Church
itself was fully capable of carrying it out.
The defect was not in the teachings of
the Church, otherwise the promises of
Christ would have failed; but the great
evil of the times was a manifest lack of
energy in enforcing its disciplinary laws.

The Church set to work in deep earnestness, in this very same sixteenth century, to bring about a general reformation
by its celebrated Council of Trent, and it
accomplished thereby the grand object in
view. "No general council," says the
Protestant historian Hallam, "ever con-

tained so many persons of eminent learning as that of Trent, nor is there any ground for believing that any other ever investigated questions before it with so much patience, acuteness, and desire of truth."

In the beginning of his religious revolt, before pride and passion had taken too strong a hold upon him, Luther himself acknowledged, in his letter to Pope Leo X., that he had no ground for separating from the Church. He thus writes : "That the Roman Church is more honored by God than all others is not to be doubted. St. Peter and St. Paul, forty-six popes, some hundreds of thousands of martyrs have laid down their lives in its communion, having overcome hell and the world; so that the eyes of God rest on the Roman Church with special favor. Though now-adays everything is in a wretched state, it is no ground for separating from the Church. On the contrary, the worse things are going the more should we hold close to her, for it is not by separating from the Church that we can make her better. We must not separate from God on account of any work of the devil, nor cease to have fellowship with the children of God who are still abiding in the pale of Rome, on account of the multitude of the ungodly. There is no sin, no amount of evil, which should be permitted to dissolve the bond of charity or break the bond of unity of the body. For love can do all things, and nothing is difficult to the united." This remarkable declaration of Luther, quoted by the bigoted Merle d'Aubigné, is surely a terrible condemnation of his own behavior with regard to the Mother-Church.

The Protestant biographer Roscoe says that Luther was treated with the greatest forbearance—so much so, indeed, that "the cause of the Church was rather injured by the condescension and moderation which he experienced."* The same writer says that "the personal character of the pontiff (Leo X.) stood high throughout all Europe. He was surrounded at home and represented abroad by men of the greatest eminence. The sovereigns of Christendom vied with one another in manifesting their obedience to the Holy See; even Luther himself had written to the pope in the most respectful terms, transmitting to him, under the title of *Resolutiones*, a full explanation of his propositions, submitting not only his writings but his life to his disposal, and declaring that he would

* *Life of Leo X.*, vol. ii. p. 107.

regard whatever proceeded from him as declared by God Himself." *

Luther, having cast off the authority of the pope, laid claim to the like authority over his own followers. He could not bear with the slightest disagreement from others with regard to his own opinions, and he gave way to the greatest violence against his opponents, supposed to be " Reformers " like himself. " Although," says Roscoe, " he was ready on all occasions to make use of arguments from Scripture for the defence of his tenets, yet when these proved insufficient he seldom hesitated to resort to more violent measures. This was fully exemplified in his conduct towards his friend Carlostadt, who, not being able to distinguish between the Romish doctrine of transubstantiation and

* *Life of Leo X.*, vol. ii. p. 95.

that of the real presence of Christ in the sacrament, had, like Zuinglius, adopted the idea that the bread and the wine were only the symbols and not the actual substance of the body and blood of Christ. Luther, however, maintained his opinion with the utmost obstinacy. The dispute became the subject of several violent publications, until Luther, who was now supported by the secular power, obtained the banishment of Carlostadt, who was at length reduced to the necessity of earning his bread by his daily labor. The unaccommodating adherence of Luther to this opinion placed also an effectual bar to the union of the Helvetic and German Reformers; and to such an uncharitable extreme did he carry his resentment against those who denied the Real Presence that he refused to admit the Swiss and the

German cities and states which had adopted the sentiments of Zuinglius and Bucer
into the confederacy for the defence of
the Protestant Church, choosing rather to
risk the total destruction of his cause than
to avail himself of the assistance of those
who did not concur with him in every
particular article of belief. Nor did Luther adhere less pertinaciously to the doctrine of predestination and of justification
by faith alone than to that of the Real
Presence in the Eucharist. In support of
these opinions. he warmly attacked Erasmus, who had attempted to maintain the
freedom of the human will ; and when
that great scholar replied in his *Hyperas-
pistes*, Luther increased his vehemence to
scurrility and abuse. ' That exasperated
viper, Erasmus,' says he, ' has again attacked me. What eloquence will the vain-

glorious animal display in the overthrow of Luther!' In defending his opinion as to the all-sufficiency of faith he suffered himself to be carried to a still further extreme, and, after having vindicated his doctrine against councils and popes and fathers, he at length impeached the authority of one of the apostles, asserting that the Epistle of James, in which the necessity of good works to a perfect faith is expressly stated and beautifully illustrated, was, in comparison with the writings of Peter and of Paul, a mere book of straw." *

Having laid down, as the very cornerstone of Protestantism, the principle of private judgment, it is not at all strange that his companions and disciples wished to claim the same for themselves, and

* *Life of Leo X.*, vol. ii. pp. 255, 256.

hence there was no end to disputes, divisions, and dissensions, even during the lifetime of Luther, whose temper was by no means thereby improved. This is well described by an English Protestant divine, the late Dr. Horne, who said: " Luther, having established the right which each individual possesses of interpreting the Sacred Scriptures, asserted too that, assisted by the light of reason, he possessed also the privilege of affixing to them their true interpretation. Admitting, with Luther, at least the former of these principles, Zuinglius presents himself, but boldly declares that not Luther but he—and long before Luther, likewise—had found out their genuine interpretation. Here Carlostadt comes forth, and, with equal intrepidity, proclaims that he has made a more accurate discovery of their real signification

than either of the above apostles ; and in-
stantly, in defiance of his master's authority, breaks in pieces the images which he
found in the churches at Wittenberg, and
excites great commotions in that city.
Not long after this these three leaders
of the Reformation commenced their disputes respecting the Holy Eucharist—a dispute in which were often blended circumstances the most ludicrous with acts of
violence the most atrocious. The champions on each side drew after them each
an immense multitude of followers in different kingdoms, provinces, and districts,
just as the pretended evidence of the sense
of the Scriptures or their pretended inspiration actuated them ; or, rather, just as
their ignorance and their passions, which
were under the control of the passions of
their leaders, conducted them."

This is a sad but true picture of the religious revolution begun by Luther and his associates. They undermined the very foundations of all Church authority, and then, strange as it may seem, were amazed to find that their own authority was likewise rejected. This was fully shown in the Protestant Synod of Dort (1618–1619), which condemned the chief of the Arminian sect and demanded submission to its decrees. The Arminians, following logically the principles of the first " Reformers," protested in these terms: " Why exact that our inspiration or judgment should yield to your opinion? The opinions of every society, our apostles, the first reformers, declared to be fallible; and consequently to exact submission to its dictates they, with great consistency, defined to be tyranny. Thus they defined it in regard to the Church of Rome, and you yourselves have sanctioned their decision. Why, therefore, exercise a dominion over us which you stigmatize as tyranny in a Church compared with whose greatness·you dwindle into insignificance? If there be any crime in resisting the decisions of our pastors, then are you, and we, and all of us guilty of resisting the authority of the Church of Rome, which existed before us, and of which our forefathers were a portion. If, indeed, such resistance be a crime, then let us altogether abandon the Reformation and run back to the bosom of Catholicity. Or, if such resistance be no crime, why require from us a submission which we do not owe you? . . . Either, in short, allow us the liberty which our forefathers claimed and yourselves approve, or let us altogether run back to the fold which they abandoned." For those who admit the Protestant principle there is certainly no escape from such a dilemma.

The greater the lapse of time from the period of the "Reformation," the more cool and impartial the judgments of thinking men become with regard to its chief characters and its influence—whether advantageous or otherwise—on the welfare of mankind. Many distinguished non-Catholic writers have done much to remove false impressions, and to place the action of the Catholic Church and of its chief pontiffs in a clearer light than was ever before exhibited.

James Anthony Froude—a bitter enemy of Catholicity—is obliged to admit that "an unfavorable estimate of the Reformers, whether just or unjust, is unquestionably gaining ground among our advanced thinkers. A greater man than either Macaulay or Buckle—the German poet Goethe—says of Luther that he threw back the intellectual progress of mankind for centuries by calling in the passions of the multitude to decide on subjects which ought to have been left to the ⁻learned." *

The majority of Protestants are under the impression that the " Reformation " brought about the emancipation of the human race from all kinds of tyranny, that the Reformers themselves were the great champions, in fact the apostles, of liberty ; while nothing is farther from the truth. Guizot, the Protestant historian of France, in his work on *Civilization in Europe* declares the contrary : " In Germany there was no political liberty ; the

* *Short Studies*, " Erasmus and Luther," p. 44.

Reformation did not introduce it ; it strengthened rather than enfeebled the power of princes ; it was rather opposed to the free institutions of the Middle Ages than favorable to their progress." *
"It emancipated the human mind," the same writer declares, " and yet pretended still to govern it by laws. . . . It did not know or respect all the rights of human thought ; at the very time it was demanding these rights for itself it was violating them towards others." Then Guizot points out the beautiful contrast : " There never was a government more consistent and systematic than that of the Church of Rome. In point of fact, the Court of Rome made more compromises and concessions than the Reformation ; in point of principle, it adhered much more closely

* Page 28.

to its system, and maintained a more consistent line of conduct."

At the beginning of his religious rebellion Luther seemed to favor human liberty; but the patronage he received from some of the ruling princes soon changed his tone, and as he advanced in years the stronger advocate did he become of despotism. The poor, wretched, misguided peasants of Germany, who simply carried into effect Luther's own principles, found in him a most bitter and relentless enemy. To give only one instance out of many that could easily be adduced, Luther, in his letter to Caspar Müller, the Chancellor of Mansfeld, says: "A rebel does not deserve to be treated with reason; we must answer him with the fist until his nose bleeds and his head flies in the air. The peasants would not hear me; we must open their ears by means of the musket. To the one who calls me unkind and unmerciful I answer this : Merciful or unmerciful, we are now speaking about God's Word, which demands the honor of the king and the destruction of the rebel." *   " I, Martin Luther, have slain all the peasants in the insurrection, because I commanded them to be killed. Their blood is upon my head. But I put it on the Lord God, by whose command I spoke." †   So much for the so-called " champion of liberty " and " emancipator of the human race."

Notwithstanding all the heresies that have arisen in different ages, and the lamentable religious secession of the sixteenth century with its most prolific

* *Sämmliche Werke*, 24, 295–319.
† Ib., 59, 284–285. Quoted by Stang.

offspring of warring sects, the Catholic
Church stands the same as ever, with its
consistent rule of faith and its invariable
standard of truth, living amid so many
changes and yet unchanged itself, and chal-
lenging the admiration of all enlightened
men, even of those who, unhappily for
themselves, remain outside its holy communion. All clear minds and earnest
seekers after truth cannot but feel its attractive power—an attraction of more than
human force—for they must feel some of
the influence of that Divine Presence always subsisting in its bosom, and calling
them to its light and grace and truth:
" And I, if I be lifted up from the earth,
will draw all things to myself." *   " Come
to me, all you that labor and are heavy
laden, and I will refresh you." †

* St. John xii. 32.   † St. Matt. xi. 28.

Professor Seelye, the author of *Ecce Homo*, in his latest work on *Natural Religion*, gives the following testimony to the attractive power of the Catholic Church : " When we try to explain the fascination which that system exerts we say : ' Catholicism is definite, has real dogmas, from which it does not flinch ; it exalts and satisfies the soul, which the cold and prosaic Protestant or rationalistic systems leave untouched.' This is the language used, but it confuses together two perfectly distinct advantages which Catholicism happens to unite. Catholicism is powerful, no doubt, because it does not explain away heaven and hell ; but its warmth, its poetic charm, have nothing to do with the inflexibility of its dogmas. These are owing to something else ; they are the reward of the firmness with which it clings to the true idea of a religion, basing its moral discipline upon true worship, enthusiastic and intimate contemplation of ideals of saintly humanity." *

The Catholic Church, then, is remarkable, first and above all, for its unity of doctrine. It is noted, secondly, for its unity of worship. This unity of worship is primarily to be found in the Mass— the sacrifice of the Body and Blood of Christ, the renewal, in an unbloody manner, of the sacrifice of Calvary, and effected on our altars in every part of the world through the ministry of the priests of the Church, the representatives of our Chief High-Priest, Jesus, the Lord. There may be, as in the East, some slight differences of rites or ceremonies, but the Sacrifice is one and the same, and by it

* Page 161.

is rendered to Almighty God a worship
worthy of Him and His infinite perfections. This is the central act of worship,
the source of perennial life to the Church,
the clean oblation prophesied by Malachy, that is offered "from the rising of
the sun to the setting thereof." All kneel
before the same altar and worship the
same God-Man, with His Flesh and
Blood, Soul and Divinity, actually present
under the sacramental veils, the appearances of bread and wine. "This do,"
said Christ to His apostles, "for a commemoration of Me."* This the Catholic
Church has done in compliance with His
commands and gifted with His power and
authority, and this she will continue to do
until time shall be no more and the
Church militant shall be transformed into

* St. Luke xxii. 19.

the Church triumphant in the everlasting abode of God.

The members of the Catholic Church are not only united in worship, but also in the reception of the same means of grace, the seven life-giving sacraments, instituted by our Blessed Lord for the salvation and sanctification of souls. As soon as our infantile eyes begin to open on this world, our Holy Mother, the Church, receives us lovingly into her arms, pours on our heads the regenerating waters of baptism, makes us truly and really the children of God and joint-heirs with Jesus Christ of His eternal inheritance. Then, after necessary instructions in the doctrines of our religion, and at an age before the passions have had time to become strong, she strengthens us in the Holy Ghost by the imposition of our bishop's hands, and we thus receive fresh strength for our approaching contest with the world and all its delusive charms, with the flesh and its alluring temptations, with the devil and his many snares.

When we have had the misfortune to stain our beautiful baptismal robe by grievous sin, she extends to us "a second plank of safety" in the Sacrament of Penance, lest we should suffer shipwreck of soul. She then leads us gently and reverently to the altar every year of our life, and oftentimes, should we so desire, during the course of each year, to be fed and refreshed with the very Flesh and Blood of our loving Redeemer.

Those who are called to the marriage state she instructs in their duties, prepares for the worthy reception of this great sacrament, and solemnly blesses their

fond union with the richest benedictions
of Heaven. Those whom the Church
deems fit to minister at her altar, and
who "are called by God as Aaron was,"
she prepares, by long years of study,
prayer, and solitude, for their high and
holy office, and endows them with godlike powers. When the moment of our
earthly dissolution approaches she anoints
with her consecrated oils those different
senses by which we have offended God,
inspires us with sentiments of true sorrow,
pours consolation into our weak, failing
hearts, brings her Divine Spouse to meet
us in the Holy Viaticum, beseeches Him
to accompany us in our approaching journey, and closes our eyes in the peace of
God—"that peace which surpasseth all understanding."

The Catholic Church is noted not only

for unity in doctrine and worship, but also, and in a most striking manner, for unity of government. Most truly is it the "one fold under the one shepherd." The Catholic laity are subject to their respective pastors, the priests are obedient to their bishops, and all the bishops of the entire Catholic world are in close communion with, and entirely obedient to, the Holy Father the Pope, the legitimate successor of St. Peter, the Rock upon which Christ built His Church, the holder of the keys of the kingdom of heaven, who has power to bind and to loose, and to feed the whole flock, the "sheep" as well as the "lambs."

As I have already dwelt at some length in a former work—*Stumbling-Blocks Made Stepping-Stones on the Road to the Catholic Church*—on the primacy as well as the infallibility of the Supreme Pontiff, I shall close this chapter by quoting Gladstone's graphic description of the government of the Catholic Church : "The Christian community under him (the pope) is organized like an army, in which each order is in strict subjection to every order that is above it. A thousand bishops are its generals ; some two hundred thousand clergy are its subordinate officers ; the laity are its proletarians. The auxiliary forces of this great military establishment are the monastic orders, and they differ from the auxiliaries of other armies in that they have a yet stricter discipline and a more complete dependence on the head than the ordinary soldiery. . . . To the charm of an unbroken continuity, to the majesty of an immense mass, to the energy of a closely serried organization, it adds another and a more legitimate source of strength. It undeniably contains within itself a large portion of the individual life of Christendom. The faith, the hope, the charity which it was the office of the Gospel to engender flourish within this precinct in the hearts of millions upon millions."

GOD is infinite holiness personified. He is the essence of all goodness, all beauty, all perfection. All His works show forth, each in its own measure, these wondrous attributes of the Almighty. More especially must this be true of His grandest creation on earth—the establishment of His one true Church, which He destined to continue, as long as this world lasts, the most important work of His Divine Son incarnate.

Hence, as the Church is the perfect image of God in His unity, so also must it be His image in holiness—the second distinctive as well as essential mark or characteristic of the one true Church. That holiness should be one of its most shining marks was, without doubt, the most earnest desire of our Blessed Lord, as St. Paul clearly intimates :· "Christ also loved the Church, and delivered Himself up for it, that He might sanctify it, cleansing it by the laver of water in the word of life ; that He might present it to Himself a glorious Church, not having spot or wrinkle, nor any such thing ; but that it should be holy and without blemish." *

To have a just, undeniable claim to the character of holiness a Church should be holy in its founder, holy in its doctrine, holy in its code of morals, its counsels of perfection, its abundant means of sanctifi-

* Ephesians v. 25–27.

cation, and holy likewise in the number of its members, whom in every age of its history it has raised to such a heroic degree of virtue as to be held and solemnly pronounced worthy of veneration and imitation. Such, we are proud to say, is the character of our Holy Mother the Catholic Church. To holiness under all these aspects she can and does lay claim; and, what is more, she is abundantly able to substantiate these claims before the world, and thus convince all sincere, truth-loving, unprejudiced minds.

Jesus Christ was the Founder of the Catholic Church. To deny this would be to deny all history, profane as well as sacred. Who, even in this age of rampant scepticism, would take it upon himself to call in question His holiness? Thanks be to God, our age is not so bad as to try to displace Christ from the position He holds over the hearts of the vast majority of civilized men. There are many, unfortunately, who deny His divinity, and who refuse to carry their cross and to walk in His sacred footsteps; yet even they are willing to admit that Christ was a most holy, a perfect Man—in fact, the model of the whole human race. So we need not linger here to point out or dwell upon the sublimity of His virtues or the perfection of His character, which have added a new, more lasting and brilliant light to this lower world—a light more beneficial as well as more resplendent than the grand, majestic orb of day, the source of life and health and vigor.

In another work—*All for Love*—the author has treated of the divine as well as of the human side of the Saviour of men.

The Apostles, or chief messengers of Christ—those whom He selected for the establishment of His Church—were men distinguished for their holiness of life. They were remarkable for entire devotedness to their sacred calling, for their absolute self-sacrifice, their patience, their fortitude and heroism amid the most terrible trials, persecutions, and harassing labors. They gave the best possible proof of sincerity by relinquishing all that men hold most dear for the sake of truth. They abandoned their ordinary vocations in life, left their families, sundered every human tie that bound them to earth, courted ignominy, suffering, and even death, for the sake of their Beloved Master and for the furtherance of that object so dear to His loving heart—the spread of the true faith and the consequent conversion of souls. They went forth "conquering and to conquer" in the name of the Crucified; their sound went forth unto the uttermost bounds, and their preaching renewed the face of the earth.

So was it likewise with those apostolic men who, at different periods of the Christian era, went forth, armed with the authority of the Vicar of Christ, to make conquests of souls for the Lord, to bring whole nations into the true fold. They were holy men, who practised all the Christian virtues, even in an heroic degree, and their sanctity was proven by numerous, well-attested miracles.

Such were, for instance, St. Patrick, the Apostle of Ireland; St. Augustine, the Apostle of England; St. Boniface, of Germany; St. Martin and St. Remy, of France, and St. Francis Xavier, the great Apostle of the Indies.

What religion, other than the Catholic, can bring forward even one example of sanctity that can, in the smallest degree, compare with these and the almost countless other saints whom we could name? Surely not even the greatest admirers of the so-called Reformers, the founders of the different sects, will go so far as to claim that *they* were *saints*. No intelligent, well-read Protestant who has carefully studied the history of the religious secession of the sixteenth century, and who has read the lives as well as the writings of Luther and his associates, would dare claim for them any degree of holiness. This is the mildest manner in which I can express it.

If we take the declarations of Luther

himself or of those who knew him well, he was very far from being a holy man, even if we abstain from all reference to his disobedience and apostasy. Judged according to the standard of the Christian Church for fifteen centuries previous to his advent, and even according to his own acknowledgment, Luther was a far better man, more moral, upright, pure, conscientious, and prayerful, before he left his monastery than he was at any time afterwards. In his commentary on St. Paul's Epistle to the Galatians he thus speaks of himself: " When I lived in my monastery I punished my body with watching and fasting and prayer. I observed my vows of chastity, of poverty and obedience. Whatever I did I did with singleness of heart, with good zeal, and for the glory of God. I feared grievously the last day, and was desirous to be saved from the bottom of my heart." Here is a different portrait of himself in after-years: "I am burnt with the flames of my untamed flesh. . . . I, who ought to be fervent in spirit, am fervent in impurity." In writing to his so-called wife, Katharina von Bora, he conveys this piece of information : "I am feeding like a Bohemian and swilling like a German, thanks be to God."

Sleydam, his favorite disciple, said of Luther : "He was so sensible of his own immorality that he wished to be removed from the office of preaching." Luther was proud, irascible, gross, and lustful. As the Rev. Dr. Brann said in a late lecture, no publisher in this country would dare publish the entire works of Luther in English. They contain so many indecencies (especially his sermon on marriage) we feel certain that Special Agent Comstock would not permit them to pass through the mail. The gentle Melanchthon said of his leader: " I tremble when I consider the passions of Luther—passions as violent as the outrages of Hercules, Philoctetes, and Marius." As to Calvin, Schusselburge says : " Horrible things are objected to Calvin in public meetings, concerning his lasciviousness, his sundry abominable vices, and his sodomitical lusts. And it was in punishment of these and of his profane doctrines that the rod of divine justice fell so heavily upon him at his death, for he died in despair, blaspheming God."

Much more could be said on this subject, and fortified also by the testimonies of those not of the Catholic faith ; for, as my readers cannot but notice, when I have anything that may seem harsh to say, yet necessary to be told, I prefer using the declarations of Protestants themselves. Such facts as these just related are not agreeable, but, whether agreeable or not, the interests of truth demand that they should not be overlooked. Charity should begin at home. Those who wish to reform others should begin by reforming themselves.

Catholics cannot but condemn the religious secession of the sixteenth century, and, in fact, every other attempt to rend asunder that unity which Jesus Christ wishes to preserve inviolate. Luther's revolt was terrible in itself and in its consequences. It severed millions of limbs from the parent tree, and checked to no small extent the spread of faith in many nations still living in " the darkness of the shadow of death." Yet it was not, after all, an absolutely unmixed evil. By its means many left the Church who, while living in it, only cast reproach upon it, more especially unworthy monks, nuns, and priests, who were only too anxious for some pretext to cast off the yoke of chastity, poverty, and obedience. Luther, whether he wished to do so or not, certainly rendered good assistance to the pope, as Dean Swift was accustomed to say, in " weeding his garden."

When the Church is fully at peace and in the enjoyment of undisturbed prosperity, there is sometimes a lack of energy, self-sacrifice, devotedness in its clergy. Soldiers who fear no immediate attack from the enemy are apt to ground arms.

Persecution is neither to be coveted nor

invited, it is true, yet Catholics cannot but admit that the Church is purer and more vigorous the more difficulties it has to overcome, the more assaults it has to bear. A body of clergy living in the midst of enemies to their faith will always be more watchful over themselves, more alert, more prepared to meet and triumph over obstacles, than those residing in undisturbed districts where the population is entirely Catholic. This is one of the reasons why the priesthood of Ireland is so highly respected and revered, even by those not of our faith. W. E. Hartpole Lecky, in his *History of European Morals*, pays the Irish priesthood this beautiful tribute : " There is no fact in Irish history more singular than the complete and, I believe, unparalleled absence among the Irish priesthood of those moral scandals which in every Continental country prove the danger of vows of celibacy. The unsuspected purity of the Irish priests is the more remarkable because, the government of the country being Protestant, there is no special inquisitorial legislation to insure it, because of the almost unbounded influence of the clergy over their parishioners, and also because, if any just cause of suspicion existed, in the fierce sectarianism of Irish public opinion it would assuredly be magnified." *

It is generally under such circumstances of trial and opposition that the highest degree of virtue is called forth and exhibited to the world. This it is that renders our clergy in this great country so active and so zealous. No body

* Vol. i. p. 146.

of clergy in the world undergoes more labor or hardship. Christian fortitude is developed by every new contest. It is thus that God turns evil into good for the sake of the Church which He came upon earth to establish, and for the consequent spiritual welfare of the human race.

The Catholic Church, then, is holy not only in its Founder and first apostles, but also in its teachings, moral as well as dogmatical. It holds up before the world and to each succeeding generation of men the same unchangeable system of divine truth, the same everlasting fact of revelation one and unalterable. It broaches nothing new, but holds up the old truths and displays them in a clearer, fuller light than before, thus opening up before our enraptured gaze side-views and fresh beauties hitherto but imperfectly disclosed or partially hidden in the sacred deposit of faith handed down by the apostles.

As to its moral code, nothing in the world is so complete, so exact, so far-reaching, or so sublime. Its code of morals is founded on the unchanging and unchangeable principles of the natural law, the Ten Commandments, the moral lessons of Christ, His precepts and counsels. Every kind of sin that can be conceived is condemned, and on every human passion it puts a check. No vice, nor even imperfection, is in any way favored. Its moral code is so perfect that it reaches the innermost thoughts of men; for Christ condemns the impure gaze and the impure desire no less than acts of impurity, as these sins are consummated in the heart: " For out of the heart proceed evil thoughts, murders, adulteries, fornications, thefts, false testimonies, blasphemies." *

Not even the simplest lie, which, when not productive of grievous injury, is only a venial fault, does the Church declare permissible, were it to save life or to avert serious injury from the Church itself. The charge that she believes in the principle that "the end justifies the means" is the grossest calumny that has ever been uttered against the Church of Christ. Satan himself could not invent a baser falsehood.

As Cardinal John Henry Newman forcibly declares : " She holds that it were better for sun and moon to drop from heaven, for the earth to fail, and for all the many millions who are upon it to die of starvation in extremest agony, so far as

*St. Matt. xv. 19.

temporal affliction goes, than that one soul, I will not say should be lost, but should commit one venial sin, should tell one wilful untruth, though it harmed no one, or steal one poor farthing without excuse." *

The Catholic Church has a special regard not only for the holiness of the individual, but also exercises a most anxious guardianship over the sanctity of family life. Hence she has always maintained, and with a steadfastness more than natural, the indissolubility of the marriage-tie. Many a terrible struggle she has been obliged to sustain during all the long ages of her varied history, many a mighty contest with kings and emperors, in order to preserve inviolate the sacramental bond. In vain did the powerful ones of the earth

* *Anglican Difficulties*, p. 190.

strive to wrest some concession from the Church on this great point. In vain they threatened and in vain they persecuted; she could never be shaken from her noble stand. Whole kingdoms were at stake, yet she wavered not. She could have preserved Great Britain to the fold, if she but consented to the passionate demand of Henry VIII. to be freed from the bond that joined him to his lawful wife; but the Church preferred to lose a kingdom than to abandon a principle.

What a striking contrast between the noble action of the Church and its Sovereign Pontiff and the truckling conduct of the chief " Reformers," who, to secure for themselves and their cause the influence of Philip, the Landgrave of Hesse, gave him permission (which no power on earth could do) to take to himself another wife

while the first was yet living ! The great
Bossuet gives us in his *History of Protestant Variations* a copy of the original
text in Latin, with a French translation,
from which we take a few extracts:
" Most Serene Prince and Lord : We
have been informed by Bucer, and in the
instructions which your highness gave
him have read, the trouble of mind and
the uneasiness of conscience your highness is under at this present ; and although
it seemed to us very difficult so speedily
to answer the doubt proposed, nevertheless we would not permit the said Bucer,
who was urgent for his return to your
highness, to go away without an answer
in writing. . . . Your highness is not ignorant how great need our poor, miserable, little, and abandoned church stands
in need of virtuous princes and rulers to

protect her ; and we doubt not but God
will always supply her with some such, although from time to time He threatens to
deprive her of them, and proves her by
sundry temptations. These things seem
to us of greatest importance in the question which Bucer has proposed to us;
your highness sufficiently of yourself comprehends the difference there is betwixt
settling an universal law and using (for
urgent reasons and with God's permission)
a dispensation in a particular case. . . .
As to what your highness says, that it is
not possible for you to abstain from this
impure life, we wish you were in a better
state before God, that you lived with a
secure conscience, and labored for the salvation of your own soul and the welfare
of your subjects. But, after all, if your
highness is fully resolved to marry a sec-

ond wife, we judge it ought to be done secretly, as we have said with regard to the dispensation demanded on the same account—that is, that none but the person you shall wed, and a few trusty persons, know of the matter, and they, too, obliged to secrecy under the seal of confession. . . . Your highness hath, therefore, in this writing not only the approbation of us all, in case of necessity, concerning what you desire, but also the reflections we have made thereupon; we beseech you to weigh them as becoming a virtuous, wise, and Christian prince. . . . We are most ready to serve your highness. Given at Wittenberg, the Wednesday after the Feast of St. Nicholas, 1539. Your highness' most humble and obedient subjects and servants, Martin Luther, Philip Melanchthon, Martin Bucer, Antony Corvin, Adam, John Leningue, Justus Winferte, Denis Melanther."

George Nuspicher, Notary Imperial, testified that he made an exact copy of the original document, which was, he declares, in Melanchthon's handwriting.

Thus was the door thrown open to contempt of the holy Sacrament of Matrimony, and that divorces should follow and increase among non-Catholics as time goes on is but a natural consequence of the evil example just cited. Professor Köstlin, in his one-sided *Life of Luther*, says, with regard to this so-called dispensation granted to Philip, that " friends of the Evangelical and Lutheran belief can only lament the decision Luther pronounced in the matter."

Marriage, outside of the Catholic Church, is no longer looked upon as a sacrament, but simply as a contract, which, under certain easy conditions, may be broken. The laws in this country are wofully loose on this important point, and the enactments of one State are at variance with those of another. All men possessed of sincere Christian feeling, and who have at heart the prosperity of this great republic, tremble for the fate of the nation. Divorce saps the very foundation of the family, and, as every one that thinks must know, when the family is undermined the state itself has no solid foundation upon which to rest.

Alliances are formed in haste, and as hastily sundered. Men are governed by whims, fancies, sudden impulses of passion, and the doctrines of free love—concealed, perhaps, under a more high-sounding name—are practically followed, Christian motives for marriage are cast aside, and Christian modesty is at a discount.

What power can stop the ever-growing evil? Intelligent non-Catholics are now willing to admit that the Catholic Church alone, with its unchangeable doctrine, can place the necessary barrier. The Rev. Dr. Morgan Dix—one of the most highly-respected ministers of the Protestant Episcopal denomination and rector of Trinity Church, New York City—bravely spoke his sentiments on this grave subject in his "Lenten Conferences" of 1883. "Moral poison," he says, "is in the air we breathe; it threatens the life of man, woman, and child; it stifles, it chokes, it makes the whole head sick and the whole heart faint; it kills and dries up from the roots the love of chastity, virtue, and honor. I am not alone in speaking on this point; I do

but repeat the words of men much higher
in position in the Church, and with larger
responsibilities. Let us hear the eminent
and learned Bishop of Connecticut. In
his convention address of 1881 he said:
'There were in the year of grace 1878, in
Maine, 478 divorces; in New Hampshire,
241; in Vermont, 197; in Massachusetts,
600; in Connecticut, 401; and in Rhode
Island, 196—making a total of 2,113, and
a larger ratio, in proportion to the population, than in France in the days of the
Revolution, though far less than in the
city of Paris. On the basis of population
by the present census there was one divorce to every 1,357 inhabitants in Maine,
one to every 1,439 in New Hampshire, one
to every 1,687 in Vermont, one to every
2,971 in Massachusetts, one to every 1,553
in Connecticut, and one to every 1,411

in Rhode Island.' Listen to some more statistics, taken still," Dr. Dix says, "from the shameful record of the New England States, which seem to be the centre of this moral cesspool. In the State of Massachusetts in 1860 there were five causes for which divorce could be obtained, and a ratio of one divorce to fifty-one marriages. In 1878 the number of causes for which divorce was allowed had advanced to nine, and the ratio to one divorce for every twenty-one marriages. In other New England States the case was even worse. In Vermont the ratio was one divorce to thirteen marriages, in Rhode Island the ratio was one divorce to ten marriages, in Connecticut the ratio was one divorce to ten marriages, New Hampshire showed about the same proportion, and in Maine it was even worse. Another fact must be stated. From the total of marriages registered in the several States those contracted and solemnized by Roman Catholics must be deducted; for they —all honor to them!—allow no divorce *a vinculo*, following literally the command of our Lord Jesus Christ. Among Protestants or non-Roman Catholics the divorces occur; and these run up to as high a rate as one divorce in every fourteen marriages—in Massachusetts and in Connecticut to one in every eight. The practical result of this facility of divorce is that in the New England States alone families are broken up at the rate of two thousand every year. And, again, note this: that while the laws protecting marriage have thus gradually weakened, and facilities for divorce extended, crimes against chastity, morality, and decency have been steadily increasing. . . . Looseness of legislation has suggested and encouraged looseness of living, and disproved the plea that sins against chastity will diminish if the law regulating marriage is made less strict."*

The Rev. Samuel W. Dike, Corresponding Secretary of the New England Divorce Reform League, says : " The great increase in the number of divorces in the last few years was a matter to excite alarm. In New England, within eighteen or twenty years, the number of divorces had doubled, far outrunning the increase in population. . . . Familiarity with the idea of divorce is increasing and working much mischief. It first permeates the lower strata of society, and gradually rises to the upper classes. Young people often marry under a deliberate

* *The Calling of a Christian Woman*, pp. 121–124.

consciousness that the tie can be loosed if they so wish, and sometimes with a deliberate purpose to do so if desirable. Thus a Vermont couple not long ago married on a probation of six months, the bargain being struck to secure a divorce at the end of that time if dissatisfied with each other. There have been a number of well-authenticated cases in Vermont of swapping wives, the divorce courts being called in to legalize the exchange. Connecticut boasts women who have been divorced from four husbands and are now living married to a fifth."

In the State of Massachusetts, according to the census of 1879, the population being 1,652,000 (from which the number of 475,000 Catholics are to be deducted whenever there is question of divorce), there were 7,223 divorces in eighteen years from 1860 to 1878. It is said that Ireland, during all her history, has not permitted as many divorces as Massachusetts in one year.

For a period covering five hundred and twenty years divorce was unknown among the ancient Romans, and the first record of one that has come down to us is that of Sp. Carvilius Ruga, B.C. 234. If there be no check to divorce in this country it will soon compare with the worst days of the Roman Empire, when women, according to Seneca, counted their years, not by the number of consuls, but by the number of their husbands: "Non consulum numero sed maritorum annos suos computant." The Rev. Dr. Dix fearlessly points out the cause of this corruption in these manly words: "The truth must be told, however painfully it may strike the unaccustomed ear. This is not only a sign of an infidel society; it is also an upgrowth from the principles which form the evil side of Protestantism. There can be no doubt as to the genesis of this abomination. I quote the language of the Bishop of Maine: 'Laxity of opinion and teaching on the sacredness of the marriage-bond and on the question of divorce originated among the Protestants of Continental Europe in the sixteenth century. It soon began to appear in the legislation of Protestant states on that Continent, and nearly at the same time to affect the laws of New England. And from that time to the present it has proceeded from one degree to another in this country, until, especially in New England and in States most directly affected by New England opinions and usages, the Christian conception of. the nature and obligations of the marriage-bond finds scarcely any recognition in legislation, or, as must thence be inferred, in the prevailing sentiment of the community.' This is a heresy, born and bred of free thought as applied to religion ; it is the outcome of the habit of interpreting the Bible according to a man's private judgment, rejecting ecclesiastical authority and Catholic tradition, and asserting our freedom to believe what we choose and to select what religion pleases us best." * No Catholic priest could say it better or make it stronger.

In the Catholic Church there is every incitement to virtue that can be conceived. Every motive, pure and strong, to perfection is constantly held up before our eyes. There is a never-ceasing appeal

* *Calling of a Christian Woman*, pp. 134, 135.

to the hearts of men to do their utmost, striving for the attainment of the highest Christian heroism. There is, in my humble opinion, no small number of Protestants who are far better than their creeds, and more exemplary in their lives than the first "Reformers" so-called. But this can never be said with truth of even the best Catholics. They can never be holier than their Church or creed; and perfect indeed they may be called if they approach in any near degree that standard of sanctity so firmly held up to men in every station of life by our Holy Mother the Church.

There are different grades in Christian perfection. There is, for instance, the ordinary way of the commandments for the majority of persons engaged in secular pursuits, for those who are more or less immersed in the things of this life, who have the cares and responsibilities of families, and who, although busied, like Martha, with many things, yet fail not to see to the *unum necessarium*, the one thing necessary—the salvation of their souls.

There is a higher life, and a higher degree of perfection consequently, to be obtained by those who, in their ardent zeal and generosity of heart, are not satisfied with merely doing what is of strict obligation, but wish to go farther in order to show their love for God and their Redeemer by following the path He traced out for them in the evangelical counsels. These counsels of Christ are, first, the voluntary renunciation of riches; secondly, the voluntary renunciation of sensual pleasures, even of such as are otherwise permitted; and, thirdly, the voluntary renunciation of one's own will—in other words, the vows of poverty, celibacy, obedience. Voluntary poverty is based on the words of our Saviour to the young man mentioned in the Gospel: "And behold, one came and said to Him: Good Master, what good shall I do that I may have life everlasting? And He said to him: Why askest thou Me concerning good? One is good, God. But if thou wilt enter into life, keep the commandments. He saith to Him: Which? And Jesus said: Thou shalt do no murder; Thou shalt not commit adultery; Thou shalt not steal; Thou shalt not bear false witness; Honor thy father and thy mother; and, Thou shalt love thy neighbor as thyself. The young man saith to Him: All these have I kept from my youth; what is yet wanting to me? Jesus saith to him: If thou wilt be perfect, go, sell what thou hast, and give to the poor, and thou shalt have treasure in heaven; and come, follow Me." * Christ counselled celibacy. "His disciples say unto Him: If the case of a man with his wife be so, it is not good to marry. He said to them: All receive not this word, but they to whom it is given." † In other words, a divine call is necessary for this higher life. "He that can receive it, let him receive it," says our Lord—*Qui potest capere, capiat.*

St. Paul says in his First Epistle to the Corinthians: "I would that all men were even as myself: but every one hath his proper gift from God; one after this manner, and another after that. But I say to the unmarried and the widows: It is good for them if they so continue, even

* St. Matt. xix. 16–21.   † Idem xix. 10, 11.

as I." *   Towards the close of the same chapter the great apostle speaks still more clearly on this subject: " But I would have you to be without solicitude. He that is without a wife is solicitous for the things that belong to the Lord, how he may please God. But he that is with a wife is solicitous for the things of the world, how he may please his wife ; and he is divided. And the unmarried woman and the virgin thinketh on the things of the Lord, that she may be holy both in body and spirit. But she that is married thinketh on the things of the world, how she may please her husband. And this I speak for your profit, not to cast a snare upon you, but for that which is decent, and which may give you power to attend upon the Lord without impediment. . . .

* 1 Cor. vii. 7, 8.

Therefore both he that giveth his virgin in marriage doeth well; and he that giveth her not doeth better."

So likewise as to holy obedience—there are those who wish to imitate their Divine Saviour still more closely by renouncing their own will and submitting themselves to their superiors in all things that are not in opposition to the law of God: " I came down from heaven not to do My own will, but the will of Him that sent Me."* " I do always the things that please Him." †

Such are the vows taken by members of religious orders in the Catholic Church. And even James Anthony Froude—bitter Protestant as he sometimes shows him- self—felt constrained to pay these self-sac- rificing religious the following beautiful

* St. John vi. 38.   † Id. viii. 29.

tribute: "They were to live for others, not for themselves. They took vows of poverty, that they might not be entangled in the pursuit of money. They took vows of chastity, that the care of a family might not distract them from the work which they had undertaken. Their efforts of charity were not limited to this world. Their days were spent in hard bodily labor, in study, or in visiting the sick. At night they were on the stone floors of their chapels, holding up their withered hands to heaven, interceding for the poor souls who were suffering in purgatory. The world, as it always will, paid honor to exceptional excellence. The system spread to the farthest limits of Christendom. The religious houses became places of refuge, where men of noble birth—kings and queens and emperors, warriors and statesmen—retired to lay down their splendid cares and end their days in peace."*

It was by means of these heroic vows, the fulfilment of the evangelical counsels, that apostolic missionaries, in every age of the history of the Church, and even in our own days, have gone forth to the most barbarous nations, carrying the cross and faith of Jesus Christ, planting the seed of His Gospel and watering it with their blood. No fear of danger could intimidate them, no threats could deter, no privation could repel, no sacrifice, howsoever great, could appall the missionaries of the Catholic Church in their quest of immortal souls. Absence from home and country, the sundering of every human tie, the renunciation of all the chief pleasures and comforts of this world, the sacrifice of

* *Short Studies*, p. 51.

health and strength, ease, reputation, and even of life itself, they cheerfully laid on the altar of God, and all this in order to co-operate with Jesus Christ in His grandest work—the salvation of souls.

Hence whatever tends to the salvation or sanctification of even one soul is of infinitely more value in the eyes of the Church than all mere material interests combined. In this she is fully in accord with the spirit of Jesus Christ, and with that, consequently, which animates the Church triumphant in heaven. She rejoices more over the conversion of one poor, miserable, despised sinner than over the completion of ten thousand miles of railway or the discovery of a hundred planets : "There shall be joy before the angels of God over one sinner doing penance." *

*St. Luke xv. 10.

All the cares and all the anxieties of the Church tend towards one most important object—the welfare of the individual soul. As Cardinal Newman says: " It contemplates, not the whole, but the parts ; not a nation, but the men who form it ; not society in the first place, but in the second place, and in the first place individuals ; it looks beyond the outward act, on and into the thought, the motive, the intention, and the will ; it looks beyond the world, and detects and moves against the devil, who is sitting in ambush behind it. It has, then, a foe in view, nay, it has a battle-field, to which the world is blind ; its proper battle-field is the heart of the individual, and its true foe is Satan. Do not think I am declaiming in the air, or translating the pages of some old worm-eaten homily. I bear my own testimony to what

has been brought home to me most closely and vividly, as a matter of fact, since I
have been a Catholic—viz., that that mighty,
world-wide Church, like her divine Author, regards, consults for, labors for the
individual soul ; she looks at the souls for
whom Christ died, and who are made over
to her ; and her one object, for which everything is sacrificed—appearances, reputation,
worldly triumph—is to acquit herself well
of this most awful responsibility. Her one
duty is to bring forward the elect to salvation, and to make them as many as she
can ; to take offences out of their path,
to warn them of sin, to rescue them from
evil, to convert them, to teach them, to
feed them, to protect them, and to perfect
them." *

No wonder, then, that such a divine

Church has produced true Christian he-
roes—real saints—in every age and in different parts of the world. Even the ra-
tionalist Lecky admits this. "It is not
surprising," he says, "that a religious system which made it a main object to inculcate moral excellence, and which, by
its doctrine of future retribution, by its
organization, and by its capacity of pro-
ducing a disinterested enthusiasm, acquired
an unexampled supremacy over the human mind, should have raised its disciples
to a very high condition of sanctity."*

Even in those ages when barbarism
and corruption weighed heavily on the
nations of Europe, when all indeed seemed dark and sad, the Church was never
without some great saints, whose lives of
purity, charity, and devotion relieved the

* *Hist. European Morals*, vol. ii. p. 11.

gloom and cast a most brilliant spiritual light on human society. Froude, the historian, gives a vivid description of the state of the Church in the thirteenth century, and most assuredly no one will accuse him of any partiality towards our religion: "At the time I speak of the Church ruled the state with the authority of a conscience; and self-interest, as a motive of action, was only named to be abhorred. The bishops and clergy were regarded freely and simply as the immediate ministers of the Almighty; and they seem to me to have really deserved that high estimate of their character. It was not for the doctrines which they taught only or chiefly that they were held in honor. Brave men do not fall down before their fellow-mortals for the words which they speak or for the rites which they per-

form. Wisdom, justice, self-denial, noble-
ness, purity, high-mindedness—these are
the qualities before which the free-born
races of Europe have been contented to
bow ; and in no order of men were such
qualities to be found as they were found
six hundred years ago in the clergy of
the Catholic Church. They called themselves the successors of the apostles. They
obtained in their Master's name universal
spiritual authority, but they made good
their pretensions by the holiness of their
own lives. They were allowed to rule because they deserved to rule, and, in the
fulness of reverence, kings and nobles
bent before a power which was nearer to
God than their own." *

Even in those dark days for the Church,
during a good part of the tenth and

* *Short Studies on Great Subjects*, pp. 46, 47.

eleventh centuries, when several unworthy men were successively forced, by the intrigue of princes, into the Chair of Peter, the Catholic Church lost not its characteristic of sanctity, for many great saints arose to point out the way to the sublime heights of Christian perfection. Such were, for instance, SS. Dunstan and Odo, Archbishops of Canterbury; SS. Oswald, Edward, Cormac, Wenceslaus, Harold, and Conrad in the tenth century; and SS. Gregory VII., Bruno, Odilo, William, Edward the Confessor, St. Margaret of Scotland, St. Colman of Ireland, St. Canute, King of Denmark, St. Stephen, King of Hungary, St. Henry II., the Emperor, SS. Romuald, Bernard, and John Gualbert in the eleventh century. In the sixteenth century (the age of Luther and Calvin) there was a galaxy of great stars in the spiritual firmament: SS. Pius V., Philip Neri, Aloysius, Ignatius, Catherine of Genoa, Teresa, Francis Borgia, Louis Bertrand, Charles Borromeo, Francis Xavier, and many others.

If, among the twelve apostles chosen by Christ Himself, one was found unworthy, it is not at all strange or remarkable that a few—happily very few—Sovereign Pontiffs, out of the long list of two hundred and fifty-eight, dishonored their high office. Some unworthy priests, bishops, or even popes do not destroy the claims of the Catholic Church to holiness; on the contrary, the corruption that did undoubtedly exist, to no small extent, in some countries at different periods of the middle ages, only showed that there was more than human power sustaining the Church— that it rested on the promises of Christ, whose words shall never fail, though heaven and earth should pass away: " Behold, I am with you all days, even unto the consummation of the world."

Had the Catholic Church been merely a human institution it could never have survived the repeated shocks of fierce persecution during the first three centuries of its history; it would have been buried under the wreck of empires, the weight of corruption and barbarism of certain portions of the middle ages; it could not have resisted the terrible religious revolution of the sixteenth century, the attacks of infidelity in the eighteenth, nor the so-called scientific onslaughts of this century. Thanks to God and His sustaining power, it shows no sign of decrepit age or intellectual weakness; it fears no attack, and not only stands its ground nobly, but is gaining strength over its enemies, and is gradually leading new nations captive under the standard of the Cross.

The Catholic Church everywhere seeks to extend her sway over the minds, and more especially over the hearts, of men. She graciously invites them to the altar of God, pours out to them from her never-failing fountains of grace her seven life-giving sacraments, all the helps they need in the various positions in life in which Providence has placed them, and she feeds and nourishes, warms and strengthens, them with the very Flesh and Blood of the Lamb that was slain from the beginning of the world. She invites all to a holy life, and generously provides them with the means of attaining it. She opens wide her arms to the returning prodigal, pours oil into the wounds of the heart, offers a solace for every woe, speaks consoling words to the sorrowful, encouraging words to the despondent, and provides homes for the afflicted and forsaken. Her priests are ever ready, day and night, "to spend and be spent" in the service of God and of our neighbor, to face contagion, to linger by the bedside of loathsome disease, and to risk life in order to bring spiritual consolation to the dying sinner. Her Sisters of Charity and Mercy and " Little Sisters of the Poor" go through our crowded thoroughfares, helping the needy and the unfortunate, and are often found breathing the air of pestilence when all others have fled in dismay. These angels of God in human flesh everywhere preach the sanctity of the Catholic Church by deeds far more powerful than words of eloquence the most sublime. Gerald Griffin well describes the Sister of Charity:

" Unshrinking where pestilence scatters his breath,
Like an angel she moves 'mid the vapors of death ;
Where rings the loud musket and flashes the sword,
Unfearing she walks, for she follows her Lord.
How sweetly she bends o'er each plague-tainted face,
With looks that are lighted with holiest grace !
How kindly she dresses each suffering limb,
For she sees in the wounded the image of Him."

Lecky admits that Protestantism's "complete suppression of the conventual system was also very far from a benefit to woman or to the world. It would be impossible to conceive any institution more needed than one which would furnish a shelter for the many women who, from poverty, or domestic unhappiness, or other causes, find themselves cast alone and unprotected into the battle of life, which would secure them from the temptations to gross vice, and from the extremities of suffering, and would convert them into agents of active, organized, and intelligent charity." * The "other causes" not specified by Mr. Lecky are nevertheless the predominating ones—viz., the love of God and of one's neighbor, as well as a desire for greater sanctification than can be obtained in merely secular life.

The Church holds up to our veneration, and more particularly for our imitation, saintly models for every station in life, from the humblest to the highest—Jesus Christ Himself being the Model of models. After our Blessed Lord the object of highest veneration is Mary, His Immaculate Mother, then St. Joseph, St. John the Baptist, the holy Apostles, and other special friends and disciples of our Saviour. There are different examples of

* *History of European Morals*, ii. p. 369.

sanctity for different stations in life—as, for instance, St. Isidore the shepherd, St. Zita the servant, as well as St. Henry, St. Edward, St. Louis, kings and emperors. They had the like passions that we have, and temptations without doubt as strong as ours, and yet they overcame them by the same means that are within our reach, and attained a degree of holiness almost disheartening for persons of our weak mould and feeble purpose to contemplate.

As Christ came upon earth "not to call the just but sinners to repentance," the Church, by means of her divinely-instituted sacraments, seeks first for the stray, wearied, wounded sheep, and, rejoicing, brings them back to the fold. She watches with special solicitude over the little lambs of the flock, whom she has begotten to spiritual life at the baptismal font. She guards these young and tender souls still more fondly in their budding years, that she may enable them to preserve their charming innocence. When reason begins to dawn, and before passion has secured a hold, she invites them to the holy tribunal of penance, where evil is oftentimes nipped in the bud, where the conscience is prudently searched, where the youthful mind is warned of approaching danger and is furnished with arms necessary for successful resistance.

God alone knows the immense good that is done through the confessional, the number of those whose innocence has been thereby preserved, the souls innumerable that have risen from the state of sin and relinquished their evil habits, the amount of injuries repaired, restitutions made, and glorious victories won over the enemy of souls.

Next to God and His blessed ones no one knows all this better than the Catholic priest. He sees not only the dark and sinful side of human nature, which many others can see almost equally as well, but, what gives him the sweetest consolations of his life amid all his trials, he has every chance of seeing the bright and holy side. He has every opportunity of discovering God's hidden saints—and, thanks to His holy grace, they are not so few in number—who have never sullied their white baptismal robe by any grievous sin, or who, like St. Augustine and St. Mary Magdalen, have made of their very sins stepping-stones to greater love, piety, and devotion.

The confessional is the great means of correction, as the Blessed Eucharist is the greatest source of spiritual life and strength to the infirm soul. No one can expect to reach the higher and holier life of the soul without frequent reception of the Sacrament of the Eucharist: "Amen, amen, I say unto you: Unless you eat the Flesh of the Son of man, and drink His Blood, you shall not have life in you."* How can those who are outside the Catholic Church, who have no altar, no sacrifice, no priesthood—how can they feed on the Flesh and Blood of Jesus Christ?

It is sad, very sad, to think of how many blessings such poor souls have been deprived, or rather robbed, by ancestors that cut themselves off from the source of unity and life. Would that they could see the Catholic Church as she really is; that they could cast aside the prejudices in which they have been unfortunately

* St. John vi. 54.

reared, and behold .their true Mother in all the splendor of her spiritual beauty, for the chief "glory of the daughter of the King is from within"—*Omnis gloria filiæ regis est ab intus*—as the inspired Psalmist declares.

The Church Catholic.

HE divine Word became incarnate for our salvation. Wishing all men to be saved and to arrive at the knowledge of truth, He likewise desired and intended that the Church which He came upon earth to establish for the carrying-out of His most gracious design should be Catholic, or universal, in its character. " Go, teach all nations " was the command given to the apostles, and, through them, to their successors in office.

This is the grand keynote of Catholicity —to teach all nations, to preach the Gospel to every tribe and race and people. All the children of men, no matter what their race or color, dispositions or peculiarities, are invited to the nuptials of the Lamb slain from the beginning of the world.

Catholicity, according to Christ's intention, was to be as truly a mark of His Church as its wonderful unity—Catholic as to time and place, Catholic as to doctrines, methods, and means, and Catholic in its most admirable adaptability to all persons, whether rich or poor, learned or illiterate, no matter in what age or clime they might live or under whatever form of government they might be placed.

Going back through the long ages, we trace the history of our holy Church to Christ, its divine Founder. To this all testimonies of any value whatsoever point. On this all history, sacred and profane, must agree; for if this one great fact be called into doubt, no event in the annals of the human race can be looked upon as certain. It is a fact that happened not in the dark or unknown to the world, and it so changed the face of the earth that it was impossible that its memory should have been forgotten or forced into oblivion.

The Catholic Church was founded by Jesus Christ—the God Incarnate—on whose divine veracity it rests as on a most sure foundation. He promised, and promised solemnly, that He would be with it all days, even unto the consummation of the world; that His Holy Spirit would always guide, enlighten, and direct it, and that not all the powers of hell would ever be able to prevail against it. It is not, then, the work or institution of man, but the special work or creation of God. It is, therefore, divine.

Other religions—if religions they may be called—are the inventions of men, whose names they bear, and the time and place of whose institution we know full well. Arius, Eutyches, Nestorius, Pelagius, Luther, Calvin, Henry VIII., John Wesley, Swedenborg, Ann Lee, Joe Smith, and many others have founded churches; in other words, have rashly attempted to improve on the work of the God-Man, and have signally failed, as all such must of necessity fail.

Every one who sets out to establish a new church or to form a new creed explicitly, or at least implicitly, starts with the assumption that Christ has failed to fulfil His most sacred promises. If the Church which He founded ever lapsed into error or heresy, if ever it corrupted the word of God or fell away—for even the shortest possible period of time—from the true faith "once delivered to the saints," then Christ was not the Son of God; He was not a divinely-appointed messenger; He was not and is not the Saviour of men; He was not a holy man, but a greater impostor than Mahomet. But if He were all that He represented Himself to be—and He certainly proved it beyond possibility of doubt by His miracles and prophecies—then the Catholic Church must stand for ever as the unfailing oracle of truth divine, the channel of grace and mercy, and the medium of salvation and sanctification unto all who will hear her voice and practise what she inculcates: "My Spirit that is in thee, and My words that I have put in thy mouth, shall not depart out of thy mouth, nor out of the mouth of thy seed, nor out of the mouth of thy seed's seed, saith the Lord, from henceforth and for ever." *

Isaias, the great prophet of God, clearly prophesied the rapid diffusion and Catholicity of the Church: " The gentiles shall walk in thy light, and kings in the brightness of thy rising. Lift up thy eyes round about, and see; all these are gathered together, they are come to thee; thy sons shall come from afar, and thy daughters shall rise up at thy side. Then shalt thou see and abound, and thy heart shall wonder and be enlarged, when the multitude of the sea shall be converted to thee, the strength of the gentiles shall come to thee." †

Other religions are merely national, like the Church of England and the Church of Russia, or are confined to one coun-

---

try or race. "We see in the English Church," says Cardinal Newman, "I will not merely say no descent from the first ages, and no relationship to the Church in other lands, but we see no body politic of any kind; we see nothing more or less than an Establishment, a department of government, or a function or operation of the state, without a substance—a mere collection of officials, depending on and living in the supreme civil power. Its unity and personality are gone, and with them its power of exciting feelings of any kind. . . . Its fruits, as far as they are good, are to be made much of as long as they last, for they are transient and without succession; its former champions of orthodoxy are no earnest of orthodoxy now; they died, and there was no reason why they should be reproduced.

Bishop is not like bishop, more than king is like king, or ministry like ministry ; its Prayer-Book is an act of Parliament of two centuries ago, and its cathedrals and its chapter-houses are the spoils of Catholicism." *

The true Church is and must necessarily be Catholic—not confined to one country or to one age, but embracing all countries and all ages. Heresy is found almost everywhere, but not by any means the same heresy or the same peculiar form of heresy. It everywhere changes its color, form, and even substance, while the truth is one and unchangeable, and remains unaffected by the peculiarities of times or temperaments, and unaltered by the vicissitudes of kingdoms or empires.

The Catholic Church is the most exten-

* *Anglican Difficulties*, p. 4.

sive as well as the most lasting of empires. The greatest dominion ever held by any secular power, not even that once possessed by mighty pagan Rome, could bear comparison with that exercised by the Church Catholic, under the control of its Supreme Head on earth, the Vicegerent of Christ, who holds the keys of the kingdom of Heaven: "I will give thee the nations for thy inheritance, and thy dominion shall extend to the extremities of the earth." St. Jerome remarked in reference to this text: "What becomes of the promises God made to His Son, that He would give Him all nations for His inheritance, if either the Church have perished or if it be shut up within the limits of an island?"

"Consider, I pray you," says the great St. Augustine, "under what folly the heretics are laboring. They, cut off from union with the Church of Christ, holding a part and letting go the whole, will not communicate with the whole world, over which the glory of Christ is spread. But we Catholics are in every nation (*nos autem Catholici in omni terra sumus*), because we communicate with every land wherein the glory of Christ is spread. . . . 'Let people confess to Thee, O God! let all people confess to Thee!' A heretic comes forward and says: 'I have people in Africa'; and another, from some other quarter, says: 'And I have people in Galatia.' Thou hast them in Africa; he has them in Galatia: I seek for a man who has them everywhere. True, because you heard, 'Let people confess to Thee, O God!' you dared to exult at the words. Learn from the verse that follows that he speaks not of a part. Let *all* people confess to Thee. Walk in the way with all nations; walk in the way with all peoples, ye children of peace, ye children of the one Catholic Church."

In his work against the Manicheans the same great doctor, speaking of the most sound wisdom of the Catholic Church, declares: "Many other things there are which keep me in her bosom. The agreement of peoples and of nations keeps me; an authority begun with miracles, nourished with hope, increased with charity, strengthened by antiquity keeps me; the succession of priests from the chair itself of the Apostle Peter—unto whom the Lord, after His resurrection, committed His sheep to be fed—down even to the present bishop keeps me; finally, the name itself of the Catholic

Church keeps me—a name which, in the midst of so many heresies, this Church alone has, not without cause, so held possession of that, though all heretics would fain have themselves called Catholics, yet to the inquiry of any stranger, 'Where is the meeting of the Catholic Church held?' no heretic would dare to point out his own basilica or house." Many of those outside the Catholic Church in this the nineteenth century of the Christian era seem as envious of the name of Catholic as the heretics of the fourth or fifth century. In the convention of the Protestant Episcopal Church held in Philadelphia in the month of October, 1883, there was quite an effort made to substitute for the name " Protestant Episcopal " that of " Holy Catholic "; but knowing full well that they had no right to a name thcy rejected more than three hundred years ago, they had the good sense to vote down the proposition by a vote of two hundred and fifty-two nays to twenty-one yeas. "The Catholicism of the Church," says the distinguished Protestant Bishop Pearson in his *Exposition of the Creed*, "consisteth in universality, as embracing all sorts of persons, as disseminated through all nations, and as comprehending all ages. The Church of Christ, in its primary institution, was made of a diffusive nature, to spread itself to all parts and corners of the earth." St. Ignatius, bishop and martyr, who lived so close to the time of the apostles as to be almost their contemporary, says in his letter to the church of Smyrna : "Christ is whcre the Catholic Church is."

The mandate of the Saviour, "Go,

teach all nations," has not been a fruit-
less one. This commission to the apostles, which has resounded throughout the
world and penetrated every corner of the
earth, has not been without its message
of peace and its message of truth. The
voices of the first apostles were heard in
many a clime and distant nation during
their lifetime, so that it was said with
truth: *Exivit sonus eorum*—Their sound
hath gone forth unto the very extremities
of the earth. They went forth conquering
and to conquer. Possessed of no worldly
influence, rejoicing not in great talents or
deep learning, supported by no secular
power, no obstacles could deter them,
no dangers appall, no sacrifices howsoever
great could intimidate them or check the
onward march of the Gospel and the consequent diffusion of our holy Church. So

wonderful was the success of the apostles and their immediate successors that as early as the second century Tertullian was able to declare to the world: "We are a people of yesterday, and yet we have filled every place belonging to you—cities, islands, castles, towns, assemblies, your very camp, your tribes, companies, palace, senate, forum! We leave you only your temples."

What earthly empire, since the world began, ever made such conquests? What kingdom or dynasty can show such antiquity or give such promise of longevity? As Macaulay well said: "No other institution is left standing which carries the mind back to the times when the smoke of sacrifice rose from the Pantheon and when camelopards and tigers bounded in the Flavian Amphitheatre. The proudest royal houses are but of yesterday when compared with the line of the Supreme Pontiffs. That line we trace back in an unbroken series from the pope who crowned Napoleon in the nineteenth century to the pope who crowned Pepin in the eighth; and far beyond the time of Pepin the august dynasty extends. The republic of Venice came next in antiquity. But the republic of Venice was modern when compared with the Papacy; and the republic of Venice is gone, and the Papacy remains. The Papacy remains, not in decay, not a mere antique, but full of life and youthful vigor. The Catholic Church is still sending forth to the farthest ends of the world missionaries as zealous as those who landed in Kent with Augustine, and still confronting kings with the same spirit with which she confronted Attila. The number of her children is greater than in any former age. Her acquisitions in the New World have more than compensated what she has lost in the Old."

We may well be proud of such a glorious ancestry, to which even the bitterest enemies of our Church pay reverence and tribute. That ancestry dates back to Jesus Christ and His apostles.

The Catholicity of the Church is imposing in grandeur and sublimity, embracing then, as it does, all times and the most distant nations, tribes, and peoples who differ in all things else—race and color, national customs, personal habits, local fashions and prejudices—and yet all agree as to the main points, the profession of the same religious doctrines, worship at the same altar, and yield obedience to the same divinely-appointed head. Thus is Malachy's prophecy fulfilled: "For from the rising of the sun even to the going down My Name is great among the gentiles; and in every place there is offered to My Name a clean oblation, for My Name is great among the gentiles, saith the Lord of Hosts."*

It showed itself to be the Catholic Church even from the beginning, not only in name but also in reality. It was unlimited by any border or territory. It claimed as its proper field the whole earth as the inheritance of Christ, and hence age after age it has brought nation after nation, tribe upon tribe, into its all-embracing fold. Even during the lifetime of the apostles so quickly did the faith spread that St. Paul could, in all truth, declare

* Mal. i., ii.

to the Romans that their faith was spoken of throughout the world.

What wonders followed the preaching of the Gospel!—preached, too, by men not gifted with human eloquence nor remarkable for the possession of any great acquirements. " Behold what follows," says Cardinal Rauscher: " The Jew, proud of his title of son of Abraham and Moses, and looking forward to the earthly reign of the Messias, humbles himself and puts aside his ambitious hopes; the Greek forsakes the splendid colonnades of the Porch and the pleasant shades of the Academy, and becomes a disciple of the Galilean; the Roman forgets the glories of his proud Capitol, and bows in reverence to the Cross; and the pagan abandons his idols and cheerfully embraces a life of self-restraint, patience, and penance. From East to West, from Ctesiphon, beyond the Euphrates, to Rome, all are become *one* people."

After the apostles had closed their earthly career the holy bishops who succeeded to their power and authority carried on the great work, and the Church began to spread rapidly over the face of the earth. For example, St. Gregory Thaumaturgus—the miracle-worker, as he was called—when he took charge of his episcopal see, about the middle of the third century, could discover only seventeen Christians within the limits of his jurisdiction; yet when he was dying he had the consolation of knowing that he left only that small number of unbelievers in that same territory, the most of the inhabitants of which he had made captive to Christ.

At the close of the third century there were flourishing churches not only in

Greece and Rome, but also in Africa and Asia. That Catholicity began to spread rapidly in Spain at an early date is evident from the fact that nineteen bishops were present at the Synod of Elvira, A.D. 306. Churches were established at Paris, Tours, Toulouse, and other principal towns in Gaul about the middle of the third century, principally through the efforts of Pope Fabian. Several of these churches claim an earlier origin, as is evident from the writings of St. Irenæus, Bishop of Lyons, in the second century, who appeals to the teachings of the churches of Gaul and Belgium against the heretics who disturbed the Church in his time.

The Abbé Faillon claims, on good ground, that Denys, the first bishop of Paris, was sent into Gaul by St. Clement who occupied the chair of Peter from

A.D. 91–101, and that St. Lazarus, whom Christ raised from the dead, became the first bishop of Marseilles. St. Irenæus declared that Catholicity had penetrated, in his time, the "two Germanies," as he termed them, and it is certain that in the third century there were bishoprics at Metz, Cologne, and Treves. "Everywhere," says Tertullian, "are to be found the disciples of the Crucified—among the Parthians and Medes, the Elamites and Mesopotamians; in Armenia and Phrygia, Cappadocia and Pontus, Asia Minor, Syria, and Cyrene, mingled with the various tribes of the Getuli and Moors in Gaul and Spain, Britain and Germany."

In the fourth century the Ethiopians, and to a great extent the Goths, became willing captives of the Cross, while in the fifth century the great St. Patrick, by commission of Pope Celestine, the successor of St. Peter, took possession of the Green Isle and brought the entire people to the Catholic faith, and established it so firmly that no amount of persecution has ever been able to eradicate it from their noble hearts. It was a bloodless victory, one altogether unique in the history of the human race, accomplished without the blood of martyrs, and there is no record of a more complete or more glorious conquest in the annals of the Christian Church. In the sixth age, although the Gospel had been preached there at an earlier date, England was brought to the true faith by St. Augustine and his companions, who were sent from Rome by St. Gregory the Great. In the same century and the age following the Netherlands and a considerable part of Germany bowed to the

Christian yoke, while St. Columba, the famous Irish monk and apostle, evangelized Sweden. Then followed the Hessians, the Thuringians, the Saxons, and the Bohemians—all coming to worship at the same altar. In the ninth century St. Cyril and St. Methodius, sent by Pope Adrian II., converted the Sclavonians, Moravians, and Bohemians. In the next century Poland was converted by St. Adalbert, Denmark by St. Poppo, Sweden by St. Sigefrid, and Lesser Russia by St. Bruno and St. Boniface.

Hungary was brought to the faith in the eleventh century, the Livonians and Icelanders in the twelfth, several tribes of Tartars by the Franciscans in the thirteenth, Lithuania in the fourteenth (Odoric himself converting twenty thousand persons), the kingdoms of Congo and Angola, besides large districts in Africa and Asia, in the fifteenth. Millions were brought over by St. Francis Xavier in the Indies, and in Mexico and Brazil by St. Louis Bertrand, Fathers Anchieta and Las Casas, in the sixteenth ; Peru, Chili, Canada, and Louisiana in the seventeenth ; and a large multitude in China in the beginning of the eighteenth century.

This apostolic work—the dearest to the heart of Jesus—still goes on, for the Church in our own times continues to send as of yore holy and intrepid missionaries to every corner of the habitable globe, bringing the glad tidings of Redemption unto every race and tribe and people : " How beautiful are the feet of them that preach the Gospel of peace, of them that bring glad tidings of good things." *

* Romans x. 15.

Even now, notwithstanding the persecution of centuries and the opposition of enemies innumerable, the tyranny of kings and parliaments, the plottings of secret societies, the dissemination of bad literature, the Catholic Church holds its own against the world and is twice more numerous than all the different Protestant sects or denominations combined. It is the religion of entire nations, such as France and Spain, Portugal and Italy, Belgium, Ireland, and Poland, the majority of the inhabitants of Austria, whilst no small proportion of the people of Germany, England, Scotland, Canada, and Australia are adherents of the Catholic Church. In the two Americas there are one hundred and eighty bishoprics and fifty-five millions of Catholics.

In the United States, where a hundred years ago we had no bishop and but a very few priests, we now count fourteen archbishops, sixty-three bishops, over seven thousand priests, seven thousand five hundred and thirty-three churches and chapels, eighty-three colleges, thirty-five seminaries, two hundred and seventy-two asylums, one hundred and fifty-four hospitals, five hundred and eighty-one academies, about twenty-five hundred parochial schools with half a million of pupils in attendance, a very large number of convents and monasteries, and an estimated Catholic population of more than nine millions.

The Catholic Church has gained a wonderful foothold in Australia, and it is rapidly growing in influence in the East, at Constantinople, in Syria, Armenia, Persia, Arabia, Egypt, Nubia, and Abyssinia. It is spread over European and Asiatic Turkey, having sixty-six episcopal sees, eleven vicariates, two apostolic prefectures, and nearly a million of Catholics. It possesses at least twenty-two apostolic vicariates in China and nearly seven hundred native and European priests.

In Africa there is a cardinal archbishop and a number of suffragan bishops. In India there are this year (1885) twenty-five bishops, twelve hundred priests, six hundred monks and nuns, and one million two hundred thousand members of our Church.

Its noble missionaries still go forth, as the apostles of old, far away from home and country, sundering every human tie, braving every danger, crossing perilous seas, entering wild forests, facing disease and death, penetrating the very heart of pagan countries, carrying no arms but the Cross, relying on no power but that of God, vowing themselves to poverty and

death for the sake of those for whom
Christ died.

It is no wonder, then, that God blesses
their labors and accepts their sacrifices.
They alone, gifted with true mission and
jurisdiction from the Holy See, full of
zeal, piety, disinterestedness, and heroic
devotedness, are able to bring tribes and
peoples to the true faith. For it is a fact
patent to all that no Protestant sect has
ever been able to accomplish the conversion of even one race. Let any one who
doubts this statement consult the learned
and exhaustive work of Dr. Marshall on
the *History of Christian Missions,* and he
will there clearly see, even from the testimonies of distinguished Protestants, that
the missions undertaken by the various
sects in different parts of the world have
been complete failures. He quotes eleven

hundred writers, of whom nine hundred and forty-seven are Protestants, and many of these the missionary representatives of the different denominations. As Washington Irving declared, Catholic missionaries labored "with a power that no other Christians have exhibited."

"Not only," says Dr. Marshall, "is the Catholic Church defending at this hour the Scriptures, the Incarnation, and the whole blessed Gospel against the ribald assaults of the 'reformed' communities, but her missions to the heathen, as her worst enemies confess, are still, both in their agents and their results, absolutely identical with those which subdued the Roman Empire to the law of Christ, and carried the Cross in triumph from Jerusalem to Rome and Constantinople, and from the shores of the Euphrates and the Nile to the forests of Scandinavia and the isles of Britain. Nay, more, the work which she has accomplished during the last three centuries, beginning from the very date of the so-called Reformation, actually surpasses all which she had done in earlier ages, even in those which witnessed her first combats with the power of evil." *

Catholic, or universal, as to time and place, the Church is Catholic also as to doctrines, teaching the same in every age, holding up the same invariable standard of truth and morals to every generation of men. She is Catholic also as to her adaptability to suit the requirements of every age, and, without the compromise of any of her well-established principles, she accommodates herself to the wants and desires of every people.

* *Christian Missions*, vol. ii. p. 405.

Being the only divinely-authorized channel of communication between man and God, she speaks with the voice of authority to all men without distinction of race, culture, or position. To the high in station as to those in the humbler walks in life, to the deeply-learned philosopher as well as to the unlettered peasant, to the king as to the beggar, she bears the same heavenly message, imposes the same obligations, holds up the same high standard of morality and the same system of divine truth.

With godlike kindness she stoops to the lowly, is condescending with the simple, tender and compassionate to the poor, and brings the proud and haughty in humility to her feet. In one word, she makes herself all to all, that she may gain all to Christ and bring them all safely into the one true fold under the one true Shepherd of their immortal souls.

Go back through the centuries; you will find the same Catholic Church existing in every age until you mount to its source or origin—Christ Jesus, our Lord. It has no other history, it is built upon no other foundation, it has no other founder. If instituted by man, whether pope or bishop, priest or layman, king or philosopher, who was he, where did he live, when did he flourish? As no more important event ever took place, there ought certainly to be some record of it. We know the history of every kingdom or dynasty; we know the names of the originators of every new heresy or schism; we can trace even their simplest variation; we know the names of the founders of the different sects, even of those considered the most insignificant; if, then, the Catholic Church has not Christ for its founder, who then founded it, when and where? Surely an event of such magnitude, having such important consequences for the human race, such remarkable influence on their temporal and eternal destinies, could not have taken place unknown to the world, could not possibly have occurred in the dark or been sprung upon mankind without some remarkable revolution in the minds of men. And yet, strange to say, not even our bitterest opponents can name any other author or founder, or determine upon any other time and place, than what we claim and always have claimed.

Moreover, when we consider that this same Catholic religion which we profess is not one that would attract the merely natural man, but, on the contrary, repel him by reason of its deep mysteries, its incomparably high moral code, and the many severe checks and restraints it places on every human passion, no mere man nor body of men could ever have been able to impose it on men and convince them that it was born of God and was fortified by His divine sanction.

In every age of the Christian era the best and noblest and most learned of men have admitted its divine origin, have accepted its teaching as the teaching of God, and have bowed down their intellects to its system of truth and subjected their wills to its code of laws. Thus it stands and shall stand for ever, until time shall be absorbed in eternity, the mouthpiece of the Incarnate God, the infallible interpreter of His revelation, the living organ of the Holy Ghost.

The Church Apostolic.

OUR Blessed Saviour declared Himself to be " the way, the truth, the life." He came to earth to point out the way, to make known the truth, to secure to us everlasting life. As His stay here below was to be short, He wished to organize a body which would surely carry out His most beneficent designs in man's regard. With this end in view He established a society distinct, definite, founded on clearly laid down principles, and governed by certain well-defined laws. This society or Church He intended not merely for the benefit of His contemporaries, but for succeeding generations of men. How long did He destine it to last? During all time—as long as there would be a human soul to be saved: "Behold, I am with you all days, even unto the consummation of the world."

Being all-wise, He must necessarily have selected the means suitable for the carrying-out of His holy purpose. Being all-powerful, He must necessarily have chosen such means as would infallibly secure the end He had in view. As He desired the salvation of men, so He chose the ministry of men to co-operate with Him in His divine work. In the Church, therefore, which He established He constituted a ministry—a ministry to teach, to guide, to govern, and direct. Being instituted by Him, this ministry is divine.

This mission and ministry He confided to His apostles, whose commission is couched in very clear terms: "And Jesus coming, spoke to them, saying: All power is given to Me in heaven and on earth. Going therefore teach ye all nations; baptizing them in the name of the Father, and of the Son, and of the Holy Ghost, teaching them to observe all things whatsoever I have commanded you; and behold I am with you all days, even to the consummation of the world."*

The mission He gave to them was similar in its nature and in its power to the one He Himself received from His Heavenly Father: "As the Father hath sent Me, I also send you."† Whatsoever they should do in His name, fortified as they were by His authority, would be ratified in the highest heavens: "Whatsoever you shall bind upon earth shall be

* St. Matt. xxviii. 18–20.   † St. John xx. 21.

bound also in heaven; and whatsoever you shall loose upon earth shall be loosed also in heaven."*

He entrusted them with godlike powers: "Whose sins you shall forgive, they are forgiven them; and whose sins you shall retain, they are retained."†

Who was to be their support, what their reliance? "Behold I am with you all days," says Christ the Lord. Who should be ever present to guide and enlighten them? "I will send you another Paraclete, the Comforter, the Holy Spirit, who will teach you all truth and abide with you for ever."‡ Who was to be the centre of authority, the bond of union, and the source of jurisdiction for this world-wide community? "Thou art Peter

* St. Matt. xviii. 18.   † St. John xx. 23.
‡ St. John xiv. 16: xvi. 13.

[or a rock], and on this rock I will build My Church." Was there any danger it should ever fail, or teach error, or become corrupt in doctrine or in morals? "The gates of hell shall never prevail against it." Who was appointed to feed the whole flock, the sheep as well as the lambs, to watch over the shepherds of the different portions of the one fold, to confirm the wavering, to strengthen the weak, to warn the wayward? None other than he to whom the Lord said: " Feed my lambs, feed my sheep."* None other than the chief of the apostles, to whom Christ addressed these remarkable words: " Simon, Simon, behold Satan hath desired to have you that he may sift you as wheat. But I have prayed for thee that thy faith fail not; and thou, being

* St. John xxi. 15-17.

once converted, confirm thy brethren." *
To that very same Peter, and through
him to his successors, the Lord gave even
the very "keys of the kingdom of heaven." To him alone, among all the apostles, was this said. The successor of St.
Peter, and he alone, rejoices in the possession of this wonderful prerogative, is
blessed with such godlike powers.

What claim have the apostles and their
successors on man's obedience? "He that
hears you hears Me." "He that will not
hear the Church, let him be to thee as
the heathen and the publican."

So we cannot but perceive that there is
not an important question that can possibly be asked with regard to the organization of the Church and its ministry, and
the chief plan of its government, that is

* St. Luke xxii. 31, 32.

not clearly answered by Jesus Christ Himself and in His own divine words.

Christ then gave a mission to His
apostles, as He Himself received a mission from His Father in heaven. As
their mission was to teach all nations and
all generations of men, and as they per-
sonally could not visit and convert all
tribes and peoples, and remain upon earth
until the consummation of ages, their mission was not to end with their mortal
life, but was to continue in their official
successors, who were to enjoy the same
powers of teaching, governing, feeding the
flock of Christ, and of building up His
Mystical Body, which is His Church.
There then exists, and must necessarily
exist, an apostolic mission and ministry
which are to last for all time.

The belief in the necessity of an apostolic mission and ministry is coeval with Christianity. In the very beginning, after the Ascension of Christ, the apostles assembled under the direction of St. Peter, their chief, who addressed them on the occasion and spoke of the need of choosing one " to take the place of this ministry and apostleship from which Judas hath by transgression fallen." After consulting with God in fervent prayer "the lot fell upon Matthias, and he was numbered with the eleven apostles." *

St. Peter first established himself at Antioch, and, after a few years, finally established his seat at Rome, the capital of the world. To deny that St. Peter, the first pope, fixed his see at Rome, resided there many years, and finally suffered martyrdom in that city would be

* Acts of the Apostles i. 26.

just as senseless as to deny that Washington was the first President of the United States. "The mass of learned Protestants," says the learned Archdeacon Farrar, "Scaliger, Casaubon, Grotius, Usher, Bramhall, Pearson, Cave, Schröckh, Gieseler, Bleek, Olshausen, Wieseler, Hilgenfeld, etc., to a greater or less degree, admit his (Peter's) martyrdom or residence at Rome." *

St. Peter consecrated St. Mark bishop of Alexandria, the chief city of Africa. St. Paul most assuredly received an extraordinary mission from heaven, yet he did not assume the apostleship until after his ordination and consecration : "There were in the church which was at Antioch, prophets and doctors, among whom was Barnabas, and Simon who was called Niger, and

* *Early Days of Christianity*, Appendix, p. 595.

Lucius of Cyrene, and Manahen, who was the foster-brother of Herod the tetrarch, and Saul. And as they were ministering to the Lord, and fasting, the Holy Ghost said to them : Separate me Saul and Barnabas for the work whereunto I have taken them. Then they, fasting and praying, and imposing their hands upon them, sent them away. So they, being sent by the Holy Ghost, went to Seleucia, and from thence they sailed to Cyprus." *

St. Paul consecrated Timothy bishop of Ephesus and Titus bishop of Crete. St. Clement (pope A.D. 100), in his epistle to the Corinthians, says : " God has sent Jesus Christ, and Jesus Christ has sent His apostles. These faithful ministers, having received the command from the mouth of their Divine Master, went every-

---

* Acts xiii. 1-5.

where to announce the kingdom of God; and, preaching thus in the country and in the cities, they chose the first-fruits of the new-born churches, and, having tried them by the light of the Holy Ghost with which they were filled, they established these men bishops and deacons over those who were to believe in the Gospel, and they ordered that after their death others equally tried should succeed to their ministry."

An heir to the throne must prove his genealogy, and surely none can show a clearer title than the successors of St. Peter. Our present Pope, Leo XIII., now happily reigning (whom may God long preserve!), is the two hundred and fifty-eighth pope in direct succession from the blessed chief of the apostles. St. Irenæus, who lived in the age following that of the apostles, gives us a catalogue of the successors of St. Peter to A.D. 177. " We can count up," he says, " those who were appointed bishops in the churches of the apostles and their successors down to us. . . . But as it would be tedious to enumerate the succession of bishops in the different churches, we refer you to the tradition of that greatest, most ancient, and universally known Church founded at Rome by St. Peter and St. Paul, and which has been preserved there, through the succession of its bishops, down to the present time." He then gives the names of all the popes from St. Peter to Eleutherius, the pope then reigning. The next list is furnished us by Tertullian; the third by St. Optatus to the reign of Pope Siricius, A.D. 384; and St. Augustine gives us a list down to Pope Innocent I., A.D. 402. And thus we can trace from one age to another until we reach the Chief Pontiff of our own day. " If an angel from heaven should say to you," writes the great St. Augustine to one of the Donatist schismatics, "'Leave the Christianity of the universe and hold to that of the party of Donatus,' he ought to be anathema, because he would attempt to cut thee off from the whole, and to alienate thee from the promises of God, and to push thee down into a party. For if the order of bishops succeeding to each other is to be considered, how much more securely, and really beneficially, do we reckon from Peter himself, to whom, as personating the Church, the Lord says : *Upon this rock I will build My Church, and the gates of hell shall not prevail against it.* For to Peter succeeded Linus ; to Linus, Clement ; to Clement, Anacletus ; to Anacletus, Evaristus." And the great doctor goes on to enumerate the succession of Roman pontiffs down to his own time, concluding with these words: " In this order of succession no Donatist bishop appears."

As the Church cannot exist without pastors, so there can be no true pastors without mission and jurisdiction. For a valid ministry are required not only true orders or valid consecration, but also a true mission, or "*the being sent*" by proper authority, and *jurisdiction*, or the charge of souls. A mission must be either ordinary or extraordinary. To be ordinary it must come through the usual channels of Church authority. If extraordinary, it must be proved by indubitable miracles.

Christ had an extraordinary mission, and He proved it beyond possibility of doubt by the most wonderful display of almighty power, by His miracles and prophecies. "If I had not done among them the works that no other man hath done, they would not have sin," * said the Lord of the unbelieving Jews.

The apostles, as we have seen, received their mission directly from Christ : " As the Father hath sent Me, I also send you." They in turn selected others to carry on the divine work, for " neither doth any man take the honor to himself but he that is called by God, as Aaron was." †

Whence did Luther, Calvin, and the other so-called Reformers derive their mission ? Not, certainly, through the ordinary channels appointed by Christ—from Peter and his successors. Certainly not from the Catholic Church, which lopped off

* St. John xv. 24.   † Heb. v. 4.

these branches from the parent tree; not from that Church which excommunicated them, deprived them of their priestly faculties, took away their mission and jurisdiction. Not from the people, who are the sources of the civil power but not of the spiritual. The Protestant divine Dr. Hooker admitted that the ministry derives its authority "in a very different manner from that of princes and magistrates," and he moreover declared that it is "a wretched blindness not to admire so great a power as that which the clergy are endowed with, or to suppose that any but God can bestow it."

Their mission was not an extraordinary one, since they were not able to confirm it by miracles. Erasmus, a contemporary of Luther and the greatest scholar of his age, speaking on this subject, said that all the Reformers together "could not cure a lame horse."

The chiefs of the Protestant sects, such as Luther, Calvin, and their associates, were not bishops, therefore they could not ordain, and could not consequently establish a succession. Even if they had been bishops a mere material succession would not suffice. Valid orders would not be sufficient without mission and jurisdiction. The different heretics who left the Catholic Church from the fourth to the ninth century had valid orders, and the Church never disputed them, nor does she now with regard to the Eastern heretics and schismatics; but they are without jurisdiction. They are not recognized by that supreme pastor whom Christ appointed to feed both sheep and lambs; they have received no commission from him upon whom Christ built His Church, who holds "the keys of the kingdom of heaven," who has the supreme power of binding and loosing, and who was divinely appointed to be the confirmer of his brethren in the faith, and whose own faith is never to fail.

This primacy of honor, dignity, and jurisdiction was acknowledged in every age of the Christian Church, being solidly founded on Sacred Scripture and apostolic tradition. In referring to the apostles the inspired writers of the New Testament always mention St. Peter first. He was the first of that holy band to whom our Saviour appeared after His Resurrection. He presided at the election of Matthias, he worked the first miracle in the name of Christ, he was the first to preach to the Jews and the first to call the Gentiles to the faith. He is the rock on which Christ built His Church, and to him was confided the care of the shepherds as well as of the sheep of the entire flock. To him alone, as we have said before, was given the plenitude of power and jurisdiction in the universal Church, and he alone holds the very keys of the kingdom.

Even in the earliest ages the successors of St. Peter exercised this power over the universal Church, and exercised jurisdiction in churches far removed from Rome—as, for example, Pope Clement over the church of Corinth, Pope Victor over that of Ephesus, and Pope Stephen over the church of Africa. No council has ever been deemed œcumenical without their approval, and at their feet all appeals have been uniformly laid. The most learned Protestants, such as Leibnitz, Grotius, and Melanchthon, were willing to acknowledge "a primacy of order, dignity, and direction over the universal Church" in the see of Rome, and to honor and respect the pope as "supreme patriarch and chief bishop of the Catholic Church."

The great Leibnitz, in his *Systema Theologicum*, gave utterance to very Catholic sentiments on this important subject: "To the hierarchy of pastors of the Church belong not only priesthood and its preparatory grades, but also episcopacy, and even the primacy of the Sovereign Pontiff, all of which we must believe to be of divine right. As priests are ordained by a bishop, the bishop, and especially that bishop to whom the care of the entire Church is committed, has power to moderate and limit the office of the priest, so that in certain cases he is restrained from exercising the power of the keys, not only lawfully, but even validly. Moreover, the bishop, and especially the bishop who is called œcumenical and who represents the entire Church, has the power of excommunicating, and depriving of the grace of the sacraments, of binding and retaining sins, of loosing and restoring again. For it is not merely that voluntary jurisdiction which belongs to the priest in the confessional that is contained under the power of the keys, but the Church, moreover, has power to proceed against the unwilling ; and he who 'does not hear the Church' and does not keep her commandments 'should be held as the heathen and the publican' ; and as the sentence on earth is regularly confirmed by that of Heaven, such a man draws on himself, at the peril of his own soul, the weight of ecclesiastical authority, to which God Himself lends that which is last and highest in all jurisdiction—execution. . . .

"Since, therefore, our merciful and sovereign God has established His Church on earth as a sacred 'city placed upon a mountain,' His immaculate spouse and the interpreter of His will, and has so earnestly commended the universal maintenance of her unity in the bonds of love, and has commanded that she should be heard by all who would not be esteemed 'as the heathen and the publican,' it follows that He must have appointed some mode by which the will of the Church, the interpreter of the divine will, could be known. What this mode is was pointed out by the apostles, who in the beginning represented the body of the

Church. For at the council which was held in Jerusalem, in explaining their opinion, they use the words, 'It hath seemed good to the Holy Ghost and to us.' Nor did this privilege of the assistance of the Holy Ghost cease in the Church with the death of the apostles; it is to endure to 'the consummation of the world,' and has been propagated throughout the whole body of the Church by the bishops as the successors of the apostles. Now, as, from the impossibility of the bishops frequently leaving the people over whom they are placed, it is not possible to hold a council continually, or even frequently, while at the same time the person of the Church must always live and subsist in order that its will may be ascertained, it was a necessary consequence, by the divine law itself, insinuated in Christ's most memorable words to Peter (when He committed to him especially the keys of the kingdom of heaven), as well as when He thrice emphatically commanded him to 'feed His sheep,' and uniformly believed in the Church, that one among the apostles, and the successor of this one among the bishops, was invested with pre-eminent power, in order that by him, as the visible centre of unity, the body of the Church might be bound together; the common necessities be provided for; a council, if necessary, be convoked, directed; and that in the interval between councils provision might be made lest the commonwealth of the faithful sustain any injury. And as the ancients unanimously attest that the Apostle Peter governed the Church, suffered martyrdom, and appointed his successor, in the city of Rome, the capital of the world ; and as no other bishop has ever been recognized under this relation, we justly acknowledge the Bishop of Rome to be the chief of all the rest. This at least, therefore, must be held as certain : that in all things which do not admit the delay necessary for the convocation of a general council, the power of the chief of the bishops, or Sovereign Pontiff, is, during the interval, the same as that of the whole Church. We are to obey the Sovereign Pontiff as the only vicar of God on earth." This is surely a most remarkable declaration, coming, as it does, from a non-Catholic source.

No church not in communion with the see of Peter can claim true mission or jurisdiction. *" Ubi Petrus, ibi Ecclesia "*— Where Peter is, there is the Church—is and has been and ever shall be the watch-word of Catholic Christendom.   Nor can the so-called " branch theory," of which Anglicans are so fond, stand the test of truth.   Those branches that were lopped off from the parent trunk have no sap, no spiritual life or energy.   They are abso-lutely dead branches; they have severed themselves from the source of all spiritual power and authority, mission and jurisdic-tion; they are utterly dried up and cannot possibly of themselves bear fruit unto life eternal.   The great St. Cyprian, Bishop of Carthage, who flourished about the middle of the third century, says: " The Church is but one, though she be spread abroad and multiplies with the increase of her progeny; even as the sun has many rays, yet but one light; and the tree many boughs, yet its strength is one, seated in the deeply-lodged root ; and as, when many streams flow down from one source, though a multiplicity of waters seems diffused from the bountifulness of the overflowing abundance, unity is preserved in the source itself. Part a ray of the sun from its orb, and its unity forbids this division of light ; break a branch from the tree, once broken it can bud no more ; cut the stream from its fountain, the remnant will be dried up. Thus the Church, flooded with the light of the Lord, puts forth her rays through the whole world, with yet one light, which is spread upon all places, while its unity of body is not infringed. She stretches forth her branches over the whole earth in the riches of plenty, and pours abroad her bountiful and onward streams ; yet there is one head, one source, one mother, abundant in the results of her fruitfulness.

It is of her womb we are born, our nourishing is from her milk, our quickening from her breath. The Spouse of Christ cannot become adulterate; she is undefiled and chaste, owning but one home, and guarding with virtuous modesty the sanctity of one chamber. She it is who keeps us for God and appoints unto the kingdom the sons she has borne. Whosoever parts company with the Church and joins himself to an adulteress is estranged from the promises of the Church. He who leaves the Church of Christ cannot obtain the rewards of Christ. He is an alien, an outcast, an enemy. He can no longer have God for his Father who has not the Church for his Mother."

Our Blessed Saviour, in His infinite wisdom, knew how strictly necessary it was, in order to preserve His Church undi-

vided, to have a fixed centre of authority
—a bond of unity whereby the purity and
unchangeableness of faith would be secured, and all schism and disunion in matters of Church government would be prevented. Hence the "branch theory" has
no solid ground whereon to rest, for how
can bodies which have ceased to maintain
vital connection with each other yet be
parts of one organic whole? It is an exceedingly foolish supposition that a branch
just begins to exist as a branch the very
moment it is severed from the parent
trunk.

Henry VIII., as is well known, separated from the Catholic Church and cut off
all communion with the see of Peter because the pope would not sanction his divorce from his lawful wife, the pure and
pious Catharine. He thereupon set him-

self up as head of the Church of Great Britain.   He made and unmade ~bishops by his royal authority, and after his death Cranmer and other prelates of the new Anglican Church took out *new commissions* from the boy-king, Edward VI., *durante beneplacito* — while his good-will should last.

Elizabeth, on her accession to the throne, *suspended* all the bishops in the kingdom, so that they would be forced to ask fresh faculties from her as head of the Church. Each prelate-elect was obliged to take an oath wherein he "acknowledges and confesses that he holds his bishopric, as well in spirituals as in temporals, from her alone and the crown royal." So, contrary to the old axiom, "*Nemo dat quod non habet*"—No one can give what he has not—Elizabeth claimed to possess and to confer all spiritual power, mission, and jurisdiction in the Church of England as by law established. This church, or, more correctly speaking, a portion of it, claims apostolic succession, and consequently valid orders and sacraments. If its divines were able to substantiate its claim, the Roman Catholic Church would as cheerfully admit the validity of their orders as it does the orders of the heretical and schismatical communions of the East.

This matter of Anglican orders has been under discussion for the last three hundred years, and no proof has been brought forward to convince Catholic theologians that there is any solid ground for the claim.

Queen Elizabeth appointed Dr. Matthew Parker the first primate of the new Anglican hierarchy, and issued a royal commission, September the 9th, A.D. 1559, to four bishops—Tunstall, of Durham; Bourne, of Bath; Poole, of Peterborough; and Kitchen, of Llandaff—to consecrate Parker bishop. Three of the four bishops refused to consecrate a priest who had publicly broken his vows and taken to himself a wife, and whose orthodoxy they had every reason to doubt; and these three prelates—Tunstall, Bourne, and Poole—were thereupon deprived of their sees and cast into prison. Bishop Kitchen, more servile than the others, promised to take part in the consecration, and was again summoned to do so two months later, but managed to be absent on the important occasion. The consecration was then to depend upon Barlow, simply *bishop-elect* of Chichester, and others of the same ilk. To remove all difficulties Elizabeth, by her supreme *spiritual power*, issued a royal *bull*, by which she graciously supplied all defects that might have existed or might possibly exist with regard to the approaching consecration. In the letters-patent was inserted the following clause : " Supplying, nevertheless, by our supreme royal authority, by our mere motion and our certain knowledge, whatever is or shall be wanting either in the things done by you under this our mandate, or in the condition, state, or faculty of you or any of you for the accomplishment of the things aforesaid, with respect to the things which by the statutes of this our realm, or by the ecclesiastical laws in this part, are required or necessary, the emergency of the time and the necessity of affairs demanding this course."

As Father Gallwey, the distinguished

Jesuit of London, says: " The Catholic hierarchy of the Church of England—the true and real bishops of the English sees—have no part whatsoever in the formation of the new hierarchy. They make no will or testament in favor of the new bishops. The new Elizabethan bishops are not their heirs either by lineage or legacy. The old hierarchy is simply thrust aside, and four men are brought forward, not one of whom represents an English see, not one of whom holds ordinary jurisdiction, and not one of whom can give jurisdiction; and they are to consecrate the new patriarch and primate and father of the Elizabethan Church. Therefore whatever jurisdiction .the new primate has comes, not from them, but solely from the authority of the queen. The queen, in her turn, derives her jurisdiction from the vote of her packed Parliament, which passed an act (1 Eliz. c. i. viii.) declaring that '*all such jurisdiction, privileges, superiorities, and pre-eminences, spiritual and ecclesiastical, as by any spiritual or ecclesiastical power or authority hath heretofore or may lawfully be exercised, . . . shall for ever, by the authority of the present Parliament, be united and annexed to the Imperial Crown of this realm.*' This, consequently, is a complete break-off from the old state of things, a thorough revolution, a beginning of a new order and a new era. Till now we have a hierarchy holding jurisdiction from the only true source of spiritual jurisdiction, the Vicar of Christ, to whom our Lord said: 'I give thee the keys; whatsoever thou shalt loose shall be loosed, whatsoever thou shalt bind shall be bound.' That ancient hierarchy transmits nothing. It is violently extinguished and leaves no successor."*

According to Anglican accounts, Parker was consecrated December 17, about five or six o'clock in the morning, in Lambeth Chapel, by Barlow, assisted by Scorey, Coverdale, and Hodgskin, according to the rite of King Edward VI. With regard to Barlow, the records of his appointment by Henry VIII. and of his confirmation by the same are to be found, but no proof whatsoever or record of any kind has been brought forward to show that he was ever consecrated. Barlow and Cranmer, as is evident from the answers they gave before the theological commission called together by King Henry, did not believe in the necessity of

** Anglican Orders, Lecture x.*

consecration, but that appointment by the king was the only thing necessary. To the king's question, "Whether the apostles, lacking a higher power, as in not having a Christian king among them, made bishops by that necessity or by the authority given of God?" Barlow, according to Burnet's *History*,* answered briefly: "Because they lacked a Christian prince, by that necessity they ordained other bishops." To the question, "Whether in the New Testament any consecration of a bishop or a priest, or only appointing to the office be sufficient?" Cranmer answered: "In the New Testament he that is appointed to be a bishop or a priest needeth no consecration by the Scriptures, for election or appointment thereto is sufficient." Barlow re-

* Vol. i. p. 201.

plied also that "only the appointing" was necessary. "They deliberately chose," says Father Gallwey, "to have such a priesthood and such a hierarchy for England as the Church Catholic would never recognize—a priesthood and a hierarchy such as Henry VIII. yearned for, that had no other title than the king's 'appoynta-ment.' Later on some of them repented, but it was too late—the child was born; the infant church was a state church, a Protestant church, a priestless church, and a bishopless church as much as the Kirk of Scotland or any dissenting body; and so it must remain. It is born in Elizabethan Calvinism; it can never grow into a Catholic Church."

The Elizabethan divines cared nothing for consecration nor for apostolic succession. They needed no altar, for they did not believe in a sacrifice nor in the Real Presence of our Lord in the Eucharist. They hated the Mass and considered it an abomination, and all "Massing priests," as they were then called, were punished by being hanged, disembowelled, and quartered, according to the new laws of the land, for celebrating the Holy Sacrifice.

Dr. Whitaker, one of the Anglican divines of that time, says in his answer to Durey : " I would not have you think that we make such account of your orders as to consider no calling lawful without them. Therefore keep your orders to yourselves. God is not so tied to orders but that He can without orders, when the good of the Church requires, constitute ministers in the Church. And the churches have the lawful power of choosing ministers, so that there is no need to take from

you those who are to discharge the ministry among us."

Thus we see that neither the Church of
England nor the Episcopal Church of
America possesses true orders, and if there
were any solid reasons to show that they
really possessed them the Roman Catholic
Church would not deny their validity, any
more than it would deny the validity of
baptism when properly administered by
those outside her communion. Were we
even to admit that they rejoiced in their
possession, Anglicans would be in no better condition than the Donatists of the
fifth century. They certainly had valid
orders, and the Catholic Church never
denied them ; yet, though they could then
count two hundred and seventy bishops,
they were cut off from the communion of
the faithful for one act of disobedience.

Their crime was one of schism rather than of heresy, yet schism was as deeply reprobated by the Fathers of the Church as any other crime of which they could be guilty.

St. Augustine thus addresses the Donatists: "You are all guilty of schism, from which most heinous sacrilege not one of you can say that he is innocent as long as he does not communicate with the unity of all nations, unless he be forced to say that Christ has deceived us regarding that Church which, beginning at Jerusalem, is spread throughout all nations."

Our Blessed Saviour foresaw that unity could not be preserved without a centre of unity, and it was for this chief reason that He built His Church on Peter, who, through his legitimate successors, would guide His Church, preserve its unity, confirm his brethren in the faith, and be the supreme shepherd of all the sheep as well as lambs of the entire fold. St. Optatus (who flourished in the fourth century), writing against the Donatists, says : " We must see who first sat upon the chair, and where. If you are ignorant, learn ; if you know it, blush ; you cannot be charged with ignorance, therefore you must know it. . . . Therefore you cannot deny that you know that in the city of Rome the episcopal chair was bestowed on Peter first, on which sat Peter, the head of all the apostles, whence he was called Cephas ; in which one chair unity was to be pre-served by all, lest the rest of the apostles should stand up each one for a separate Church ; *so that he should be a schismatic and a sinner who should set up against the one chair another*."

This is the rock made immovable by Christ's almighty power. No waves of error, heresy, or schism can ever submerge it. Storms may rage against it, darkness may hover around it, tempests, stirred up by the passions of men or the envy of hell, may assail it on every side, yet it has its foundations in the everlasting hills, and it will remain the only refuge, the only place of safety for the poor, bewildered mariners on the stormy sea of life, who are too often tossed about by every wind of doctrine, and who will seek elsewhere in vain for any solid ground whereon to stand.

There is now, and has been for a long time, among no small number of earnest Christians a desire for unity. They cannot but see the evils of a divided Christendom—evils which have been growing more and more apparent every year. It has been the greatest obstacle to the spread of the Gospel and to the consequent salvation of barbarous nations. The answer which missionaries of different denominations invariably receive from intelligent pagans whom they seek to convert to Christ is, "Go home, and when you agree among yourselves, then come and preach to us."

This disunion is the chief cause of the indifference of the age. It has weakened the faith in many minds, and has entirely eradicated it from many hearts. It has produced that most terrible of all delusions—namely, that it matters not what a man believes, and that dogmas or eternal truths are things of no consequence. Thus religion is undermined and morality loses its sanction.

Where is the remedy? The only remedy

is the one provided by God. Certainly Christ foresaw all this disunion and its terrible consequences, and He established His Church on such a basis that, if men would heed its warnings and listen to its voice, no heresy or schism could make any headway. "He who hears you," Christ said to the rulers of His Church, "hears Me; he who despises you despises Me."

But some persons may say: "We are anxious for union, but the Catholic Church will make no concessions; it is unwilling to compromise, it is entirely too dogmatic, and, above all, it claims to be infallible in its teaching." These persons are right in their surmises. The Catholic Church cannot possibly compromise even one of its principles. It cannot make any concession to error, heresy, or disobedience. It is and must be essentially dogmatic. It claims, and cannot do otherwise than claim, infallibility, otherwise it could not be the Church of Christ. It must remain what He made it. It rests upon His unfailing promises. It is guided by His Holy Spirit, who teaches it all truth necessary to be known, and who is to remain with it, enlightening and directing it, until time shall be no more.

It cannot change its system of divine truth to please any age or any man or body of men. God's truth remains the same for ever.

Being the only true Church of Christ, it must be, like Himself, unchangeable in its standard of doctrine and morals. It can add nothing to, nor take away aught from, the deposit of faith, the truths taught by Christ or handed down by the apostles, who were inspired by the Holy Ghost. There is no new revelation to be expected. Truths may in course of time become more developed, be seen in clearer light, be defined in plainer and more forcible terms, but there can be no new doctrine. The Church cannot teach anything erroneous or heretical; it cannot lead men astray; it cannot deceive them as to the means necessary for salvation; it cannot, as a Church, become corrupt or corrupting, otherwise the promises of Christ would thereby fail, and the entire structure of Christianity would fall to the ground.

Christ established His Church on the firm, unshaken basis of one fold under one shepherd. To that shepherd, His Vicegerent on earth, St. Peter and his successors, He confided His whole flock: " Feed My lambs, feed My sheep."

" Thou art Peter [a rock], and upon this rock I will build My Church, and the gates of hell shall not prevail against it. To thee I will give the keys of the kingdom of heaven. And whatsoever thou shalt bind upon earth shall be bound also in heaven; **and** whatsoever thou shalt loose upon earth shall be loosed also in heaven." *

Surely Christ never spoke in vain, and no more remarkable words ever fell from His sacred lips than these just quoted. They are certainly clear and precise and full of the deepest meaning. It is to be feared that many of our separated brethren do not reflect upon their great significance.

Protestants say that Catholics attribute too much power to the pope. We do

* St. Matthew xvi. 18, 19.

not concede to him any more than Christ Himself does. To St. Peter alone, as head of the Apostolic College, and, as the Church was not to end with St. Peter, to his successors in office, our Divine Lord gave the very "*keys of the kingdom of heaven.*" If you do not recognize Peter in his legitimate successors, if you dispute his power and reject his authority, how can you, with any show of reason, expect to enter the heavenly portals? There is only one set of keys, and it is not in the power of man to duplicate them.

This, you may say, is intolerance, want of charity. Truth is and always must be intolerant of error. If you believe in your heart that you are strictly honest, you will be intolerant of any opinion to the contrary. You are convinced that two and two make four, and no sane man will tolerate the opinion that two and two make five.

Truth is necessarily intolerant, but not persecuting. Neither is it a want of charity to insist upon true Catholic doctrines, to proclaim them to the world frequently and forcibly.

Any man who believes most firmly that he is in possession of the only true saving faith, and who loves his fellow-men with a deep, abiding love, cannot but desire most earnestly that others may enjoy the same great gift, the same blessed privilege. We are commanded to love our neighbor as ourselves, and any one who sees his neighbor in grievous danger, whether of soul or body, and will neither warn nor help him, makes void the law of Christ.

Out of this Christian love—which we all should have one for another—these pages are written. The writer believes, with all the sincerity of his soul, that if those outside our communion would know the Catholic Church as it really is, and not as it is misrepresented; if they could but see its resplendent beauty, perceive the logical connection of its system of doctrines, the astonishing purity and loftiness of its moral code, the infinite reasonableness—if I may so express it—of its claims on man's obedience, and its wonderful adaptability to all the wants and desires of the human heart, there are thousands who would never rest satisfied until they would be admitted to its fold.

Although the attention that is given to the Catholic Church in our times is ever on the increase, yet the vast majority of our American people are in deep ignorance of its true teaching. This is also true of many persons who are in all other respects fairly educated. Even quite lately the writer has met prominent men who had the most mistaken notions with regard to the simplest truths of our religion, and who were imbued with prejudices that we had hoped had long since been dissipated—such, for instance, as that most silly and unfounded of all notions that priests were paid for the forgiveness of sins and the granting of indulgences to commit sin. Such persons must have a very poor opinion of the intelligence as well as of the morality of their Catholic neighbors. They should consider that Catholics are not fools —as fools, without doubt, they would be if they believed such doctrines as those imputed to them.

In every walk of life Catholics can be found who are at least the equals of their Protestant fellow-citizens in breadth of mind, in sharpness of intelligence, logical precision, and last, though not least, in the elevation of high moral principle. Hence it is an insult to charge them with believing what is opposed to common sense itself.

All this comes from the atmosphere of prejudice and bigotry in which so many outside the Church are unfortunately reared. The majority of Protestants seem to be afraid to enter a Catholic church or to read a Catholic book. They judge us by the declarations of our enemies. They have oftentimes been taught that it is wrong, that it is sinful, to examine the claims of the Catholic Church, that it would be a source of danger to their souls.

Their conscience is consequently an erroneous one; they cannot act against it, yet they should labor to inform and correct it.

As it is a fundamental principle of Protestantism to examine every doctrine and to follow private judgment, all we ask of those outside the household of faith is to examine well and to pray fervently; to examine our doctrines, not as they are misrepresented by our enemies, but as they are explained by our authorized teachers or by well-informed Catholics. It is not fair to ask illiterate Catholics for a reason for the faith that is in them. They know the chief principles of their religion, and very often have true ideas of its principal doctrines, but it requires education to be able to impart the knowledge which they possess.

Then, before all and above all, non-Catholics should pray earnestly, fervently, perseveringly for the light and grace of the Holy Spirit, that they may find the truth, and, when they have found it, that they may be ready and willing to embrace it, at any sacrifice; for "what doth it profit a man if he gain the whole world and lose his soul?"

There is no possibility of salvation for those who know or have reason to know that the Catholic Church is the only true Church of Christ, and yet from worldly motives will not enter it. "He who denies Me before men," says the Master, "him shall I deny before My Father who is in heaven."

They who are in serious doubt with regard to their religion are obliged in conscience to examine and thus to discover on what ground they rest their hopes.

Salvation is a matter of the greatest importance; therefore religion should not be a matter of indifference. An eternity of happiness is at stake, and, as we cannot return from the everlasting shore to rectify a mistake, so it is the duty of every one to choose the surest and safest path.

I doubt not, however, that there is a goodly number of Protestants who are in good faith and invincibly ignorant of the claims which the Catholic Church has upon their belief and obedience. If they have been validly baptized and are animated with piety and charity towards God and man, if they be sincerely sorry for all their sins out of pure love of God, if they live up to all the light they have and would embrace the Catholic faith did they but know it to be the only true one, such persons belong to the soul of the Catholic Church, and will therefore be saved.

What that eminent divine and holy prelate, Cardinal Manning, says of the good faith and invincible ignorance of the people of England can, I think, be said with scarcely less truth of the majority of American Protestants, more especially of those who live in the country districts: "The doctrine, '*extra ecclesiam nulla salus,*' is to be interpreted both by dogmatic and by moral theology. As a dogma, theologians teach that many belong to the Church who are out of its visible unity; as a moral truth, that to be out of the Church is no personal sin, except to those who sin in being out of it. That is, they will be lost, not because they are *geographically* out of it, but because they are *culpably* out of it. And they who are culpably out of it are those who know—or might and therefore ought to know—that it is their duty to submit to it. The Church teaches that men may be *inculpably* out of its pale. Now, they are inculpably out of it who are and have always been either physically or morally unable to see their obligation to submit to it."

The eminent writer then speaks of the different classes that come under this head, and "of such simple persons it may be said that *infantibus æquiparantur*—they are to be classed morally with infants. Again, to these may be added the unlearned in all classes, among whom many have no contact with the Catholic Church or with Catholic books. Under this head will come a great number of wives and daughters whose freedom of religious inquiry and religious thought is unjustly limited or suspended by the authority of parents and husbands. Add, lastly, the large class who have been studiously brought up, with all the dominant authority of the English tradition of three hundred years, to believe sincerely, and without a doubt, that the Catholic Church is corrupt, has changed the doctrines of the faith, and that the author of the Reformation is the spirit of holiness and truth. It may seem incredible to some that such an illusion exists. But it is credible to me, because for nearly forty years of my life I was fully possessed by this erroneous belief. To all such persons it is morally difficult to discover the falsehood of this illusion. All the better parts of their nature are engaged in its support; dutifulness, self-mistrust, submission, respect for others older, better, more learned than themselves, all combine to form a false conscience of the duty to refuse to hear anything against 'the religion of their fathers,' 'the church of their baptism,' or to read anything which could unsettle them. . . . Nothing that I have said above modifies the absolute and vital necessity of submitting to the Catholic Church as the only way of salvation to those who know it, by the revelation of God, to be such." *

Now that the Catholic Church is spreading more and more throughout the length and breadth of our immense country, and churches, schools, convents, and monasteries are springing up on every side, and the press of the country is treating us with greater fairness than ever before,

* *England and Christendom*, p. 91.

the chances for invincible ignorance are becoming less day by day.

It is no doubt difficult for those who were born, it might be said, in the faith to understand how there can be any earnest, intelligent persons outside the fold, when the marks of the divinity of the Roman Catholic Church are so striking and resplendent. Its remarkable unity, holiness, catholicity, and apostolicity cannot but impress the world. More especially is this so when we consider the hundreds of millions of human beings, so different in all things else, yet reciting the same unalterable creed; living in the midst of constant changes, yet still holding the same substantial faith once delivered to the saints; all worshipping at the same altar and partaking of the same divine sacraments, and all, whether rich or poor, learned or unlearned, bowing in humble submission to one divinely-appointed chief of the visible Church of God, the legitimate successor of the fisherman of Galilee, to whom is confided the highest of trusts, the weightiest of responsibilities, the most exalted of powers and dignities.

And how intensely grateful we of the Catholic faith ought to be to God for His unspeakable mercies and favors, not the least of which is the blessing which He has conferred upon us in the selection of the great Pontiff who now so worthily sits on the chair of Peter—Pope Leo XIII., whose admirable wisdom and prudence have won the admiration of the greatest men of our time, even of those who profess not our holy religion. Inflexible in principle, gentle yet firm in action, resplendent by his virtues, gifted with all the learning of the schools, fully abreast of the scientists of the age, and supreme teacher of the highest of sciences, he labors day and night to enlighten society and to bring back to the fold all those who have wandered far away from the source of true light and knowledge and are lost in the labyrinth of materialism and infidelity.

May the Almighty long preserve to the Church our great Pontiff, Leo XIII., and may God crown his declining days by as miraculous draught of the souls of men as would gladden the heart of St. Peter himself, the first of that glorious line of "fishers of men" who hold by right divine the "Keys of the Kingdom of Heaven"!